INHERITANCE

PILLARS OF MAGIC: DOMINION CHAPTER

LISSA KASEY

Inheritance : Pillars of Magic: Dominion Chapter

2nd Edition

Copyright © 2015 Lissa Kasey

All rights reserved

Cover Art by Doelle Designs

Published by Lissa Kasey

http://www.lissakasey.com

TRIGGER WARNING

Listed below are the trigger warnings for this book. If any of these things bother you, please proceed with caution:

- References to sexual assault on a minor
- Sexual assault and coercion
- Memories of child abuse/neglect
- Mental illnesses including OCD, Anxiety, Depression, Codependency, and Mania

PROLOGUE

I pulled on a pair of nice jeans and a semi-sheer sweater. There was no point in dressing up too much since the clothes would be on the floor in less than an hour anyway, as long as I could convince Gabe that fucking was better than a movie at home. When he called yesterday to ask me out, that's more what I had in mind, but had agreed to dinner and a movie anyway.

I locked the door to my dorm room and glanced around, hoping that no prying eyes followed me. The whole building was co-ed, and more than half of the residents were witches. Female witches were the norm and made up the entirety of the Dominion, the governing body of magic. I had the misfortune to be the only male on campus studying magic, but since I was the last living witch in the Rou line—my mother was the regional director of the Midwest Dominion branch—I had to break the boundaries or my mom would kill me.

The girls tried to drive me out through pranks and teasing, just to prove that guys couldn't be witches. History proved that men just weren't as powerful as females when it came to magic—most men. I wasn't most men. It was why I had a single room to myself: no one wanted to bunk with the pariah of the whole campus.

So far all the pranks had been minor. Nasty notes slipped under my door, people tripping me in the hall or pushing me whenever they passed, lots of name-calling and reporting me to teachers for things I hadn't done. I could handle it. It was all kid stuff.

"Hey, Seiran."

I turned around, expecting someone to throw something or curse my existence. Ryan Federoff—one of the offensive linemen for the football team—lingered in the hall. He was in my math class but had never said more than two words to me. In fact, he hung with some of the witches who spent a lot of time tormenting me, like Rose Pewette, who was the Pillar of earth. She seemed to take the "mean girl" concept to a whole new level.

"Hi," I said carefully as I waited for the punch line and hoped it wasn't my face.

He smiled and his face lit up, easing some of my anxiety. "Going out?"

"Just for a while. Meeting a friend." I tried to be casual. Ryan was cute in that rugged sports-star sort of way. Long face with lots of angles and a bulky body—probably from steroids—but he wasn't unattractive. He was sort of considered a catch by most of the Dominion girls since he came from a Dominion family. Good bloodlines and all that crap. Sometimes I wondered if they were breeding horses with the way everyone talked about who should mate with who to beget what. It was a relief to be gay and not have to worry about the baby gig. Life was enough stress without all that hassle.

Ryan crossed the hall as I headed for the door. He fell in step with me. "A date? Is it serious?"

Was he hitting on me? The guys at school rarely spoke to me. Ryan couldn't have known me well enough to know that I didn't date seriously, but I didn't want to give him the impression that I was easy either.

I gave him a wide, but fake, smile. "Just meeting a friend."

"Call me sometime and we can get a drink." He touched my arm and ran his fingers down the edge of my sweater's soft fabric until they reached my wrist—like he was going to take my hand. It was an odd move. Did he think 'cause I looked like a girl that he had to treat me like one? My long hair did not mean I liked flowers and long walks on the beach—long fucks on the beach maybe…

"Sure." I didn't mention to him that I wasn't old enough to legally drink in public, but he wasn't really looking for conversation over alcohol anyway. His body language said sex in a thousand different ways. He'd do for a one-off some night I didn't want to leave campus. It was college after all. The time to explore the world and our sexuality. Maybe he'd never been with another guy. I wasn't really good at breaking in firsts, but I'd give it the old college try. But not tonight. I'd already made a promise.

He gave me his number and walked me to my car, seeming very gentleman-like for a jock. "Later," he said.

"Later," I told him and watched him head off down the path leading to some of the other dorms. I felt like someone was watching me. It was a heavy apprehension weighing at my shoulders. I tried to shrug it off, but the unease that tingled a warning down my spine had become a way of life. I'd have to hit the books harder to see if there was a spell that could tell me if I was paranoid or really being stalked by someone. I preferred the former.

I unlocked my car, sighing at its broken-down exterior. My meager savings from mowing the neighbors' lawns and walking pets had paid for the car. My mother gave me enough money for food and gas each month. It was at her insistence that I studied magic. Her coercion had been the kind I couldn't say no to since she could be very demanding. Living on campus had been my only chance to escape her constant supervision, but I'd traded one prison for another. Some days I wondered if there would ever be an end.

Only two things really helped me find peace: sex and shifting into my lynx form to run free on the new moon. The second was illegal by Dominion law. Witches were not allowed to shift, since —unlike lycanthropes—they had a tendency to not want to return to human form. But sex could be easily procured, as I planned to do tonight. Gabe was always a pretty sure thing, ever since I became legal. And if Gabe wasn't up for play, apparently I had a backup plan in Ryan Federoff.

Unlike on campus, I'd be safe from scathing glances at Gabe's. He was a two-thousand-year-old vampire. Anyone who messed with him deserved to have their throat torn out.

I drove to Gabe's and parked in the lot of his condo, beneath the light, and hurried to the door. Somehow the unease had followed me, at least until I rode the elevator up to his loft. The door was cracked open for me—he could do that because he lived in a secure building on the good side of St. Paul.

His place was all wooden floors, granite counters, and endless windows that overlooked the city skyline. Beautiful, if you liked that sort of thing. As an earth witch, I preferred trees, but who was I to tell a vampire how to live?

The first thing that hit me when I entered was the breeze from the open balcony door. We rarely went outside at this height, and because it was late October, the wind was a little more than cold. Usually we retired quickly to the loft above, where his king-sized bed would be turned down for the night. Or he'd fuck me into the wall beside the door or sometimes even on the kitchen counter. Wherever was fine with me so long as we got on with it.

He'd been my only repeat, the only guy I ever came to more than once. I didn't know if it was because of his pretty words, his firm round ass and amazingly sculpted shoulders, or the lack of fear I had when in his arms. Either way, my body seemed to really like everything he did, and my commitment-phobic head didn't gripe too much. As long as he didn't mention the *L* word.

"Hey," Gabe said, his slightly accented voice coming from the balcony doorway. He stood in a casual, cover-model pose with strong arms crossed over his chest. And he looked like a model with his blond hair in an array of curls and green eyes glowing with a light of happiness that I only got to see on rare occasions.

"We're watching a movie on the balcony?" I crossed the room, stripping off my shirt as I moved, showing off my flat stomach and ever-ready nipples. Maybe I'd get them pierced, attract more attention to them. No one ever touched them as much as I'd like. I'd never have a six-pack, just didn't have the right body type for it, but I could work with what I had.

I reached him and stretched up on my tiptoes to kiss his lips lightly. He pulled me in closer, pressing a hand at the back of my neck, weaving his fingers through my long black hair, and slipping his tongue into my mouth to duel with mine.

"Hmm," I sighed happily into his lips.

He pulled away and stroked my cheek, looking so serious for a minute it brought on a sense of panic. If he said the words, I'd be out the door. But he knew that. It had happened before. So he just said, "You look great."

I rubbed my erection against his thigh to remind him that I felt great too. "Can we skip the movie?"

"I made you dinner." He pulled away and headed out onto the covered balcony where a small table sat decked out like one from some sort of fancy restaurant. White tablecloth, red roses, fancy plates, and a cart beside it that was sure to be filled with gourmet cuisine.

The whole sight made me cold. "What is this?"

"Just dinner." He motioned toward the chair. I hesitantly took a seat and watched as he served the meal. After he returned to his seat, I picked up my fork and dug in to the yummy-looking dinner. The salmon was moist and flaky in a rich cheese sauce with steamed vegetables and a flavorful couscous mix. Gabe poured wine for both of us, a soft white that tickled my palate nicely with the taste of the food.

I dug in while he studied me. He sipped at his own glass of wine, swirling it occasionally, and tapped his fingers lightly on the table. Gabe wasn't usually so physically animated. He was more of a talker. His silence was beginning to make me nervous.

Finally I put my fork down and stared at him. "What's going on?"

He shook his head. "Nothing."

"So what's the deal with the romantic dinner, then?"

"No deal. I just wanted to spend a nice evening with you. One that didn't just revolve around sex." He got up and went to the cart. "Ready for dessert?"

Dessert was simple. Fresh vanilla ice cream with strawberries and chocolate poured over the top. He set the dish in front of me and returned to his chair. Instead of putting my spoon in and going to town on the sweet treat, I picked it up and moved to his side of the table. He slid back enough to let me plop into his lap, then held my dessert bowl for me. I dipped my spoon into the concoction, hoping to get this evening moving in a more familiar direction.

I sucked on the spoon, swirled the cream around in my mouth before swallowing, and pressed my lips to his. Gabe didn't hesitate to let me in and then deepened the kiss. His normal flavor tinted with wine made me smile into his mouth. He cupped my ass with his free hand, and I massaged his neck and cheek with mine. He offered me the bowl, encouraging me to take another sugary spoonful, and I did, lapping and sucking at the spoon, playing with it to find every drop. Our eyes were locked to each other's—mine probably as lust-filled as his. His erection ground into my thigh, and mine begged to be touched.

The chilly Minnesota air made me shiver. "Let's take this inside," I said, slipping off his lap and tugging him away from the table. He left the bowl there and followed me, pressing kisses to my hair as we went.

We only made it as far as the stairs to the loft before he shoved me against them, unbuttoned my pants, and slipped his hands inside. I sighed as his warm grip enveloped me.

"Heavy on the QuickLife tonight, eh?" I said, meeting his endless kisses. The bottled synthetic blood staved off his hunger and kept his temperature up and ready even when I wasn't feeding him.

"Always prepared for you," he breathed against my skin. He bathed my neck and chest in kisses. When he finally reached my aching nipples and sucked one into his mouth, I arched against him, throwing my head back in ecstasy.

When he moved to the other nipple, I reached up to run my hands through his hair. I hated the smell of his stinky herbal shampoo, but it was so *him* I couldn't complain much about it. As he bowed his head to reach my nipple, something across the room caught my eye.

A wall calendar pinned up beside the door had big red Xs marked over each day of the month until today, which was circled. Gabe kissed down my stomach. I tugged gently at his hair. "What's today?"

"Hmm?" he answered. "October twenty-sixth."

"I know the date. But why do you have it circled on your calendar?"

He sat down on the stair beside me, still rubbing my lower abdomen. "Older vamps like me have a hard time keeping up with dates. So I have to write things down."

That still wasn't an answer. He tried to kiss me again, but I pushed him away and crossed the room to look at the calendar. Did he have something important today that he didn't tell me about? Why did he insist we go out tonight, on a Tuesday of all nights, if he had other things going on? Written in the big red bubble was *Anniversary*.

My heart jumped faster in my chest, and my mind raced to recall the dates, but all I remembered about that Halloween party was that it had been on a new moon two years ago, when I was sixteen. Panic took hold of me as Gabe wrapped his arms around me from behind. "It's nothing, Sei. Let's go to bed."

"What anniversary?"

His silence was answer enough.

I tore myself out of his arms and grabbed my shirt. "The anniversary of when we first met?"

"Why is that a bad thing, Sei?"

I shrugged the shirt over my head and rubbed my eyes. "Anniversaries are for couples."

"They're for friends too. We *are* friends, aren't we?"

"Friends who fuck. Not friends who celebrate the day they met. What's next, the celebration of the first time you did me?" My lungs tightened and I could almost feel the world closing in around me. Relationships and I did not work. Gabe deserved better anyway. There was so much about me that he didn't know. It was better if he just thought of me as an indiscriminant slut.

"Don't make this more than it needs to be, Sei. I just wanted to spend the night with you—"

"You're the one who made it more than it needed to be. Fancy dinners, flowers, what else were you planning? Asking for a domestic partnership during the afterglow?" The idea nearly brought me to my knees. Didn't he realize that he'd get tired of me if I stuck around?

I couldn't stay. The hope in his eyes made my heart break. When he learned who I really was, he'd hate me, and I couldn't bear that. I wouldn't expose him to my fucked-up head.

I stomped to the door. "Don't call me."

"Sei…."

"Find someone else to play house with you, Gabe. I'm going to find someone to fuck me." I slammed the door, feeling childish, but couldn't help it. I wouldn't really find someone else, since my heart was racing and I needed some time to calm down, but he just made me so mad sometimes.

My whole body shook as I made my way down to my car. The tremors had started after my mom got the promise from me that I'd attend the university and study magic. It was getting worse all the time. I wondered how much longer I could hide it. The world seemed to be falling apart around me. People hated me at school, I couldn't go home to my mother, and now I didn't even have Gabe to rely on for occasional, comforting, uncomplicated sex.

I started the car and took off for the dorm. Once there, I went in only to grab a book, then headed out on foot toward the all-night café near the library. At least this late at night, I could probably find a nice hidden corner to relax for a while.

When I was halfway to the café, someone stepped onto the path, and I ran right into a broad chest. He grabbed my arm to steady me. "Sorry," he said.

"S'okay," I told him. He was a big guy, probably over six feet tall, with long blond hair, and he wore a heavy jacket. He smelled of strong deodorant and a spicy aftershave. I had to rub my nose to keep from sneezing. Stupid oversensitive sense of smell.

"Can I walk you somewhere? It's pretty late."

I moved around him and headed toward the café. "I'm fine, thanks." When he didn't follow, I let out a heavy sigh of relief. Why had I become so jumpy? I had sex with vampires, lycanthropes, and humans. Any one of the batch could easily hurt a small guy like me, but instead it was the dark that made me afraid. Where was the logic in that?

The café was a welcoming light in the distance. When I finally reached the door and went inside, I felt safe again. I ordered a cup of hot cocoa and found a nice little corner table. The barista knew me well enough to come over and wipe down the table for me.

I gave her a strained smile and opened my book to get lost in a hot romance with man-on-man action. The main character was lavishing attention on his lover's silken, turgid rod and playing with the puckered skin of his love hole, when the chair across from me screeched and someone dropped into it. I glanced up, blinking to focus on the bigger picture of the room.

Ryan sat across from me. "Hey."

"Hey."

"Meeting your friend here?"

"No. Saw him earlier. That's over." I looked back down to my book, not really in the mood for sex anymore. Maybe another night. Hopefully Ryan would get the point.

"It's almost 1:00 a.m."

"Yeah. It's late."

"Can I walk you home?"

I stifled a sigh. Why did everyone think I needed to be walked home? Was he that hot for me? He didn't seem like the kind of guy who had to beg. I shrugged. "Sure." I bookmarked my page, got up, and pushed in my chair.

He motioned for me to go ahead of him and waited for me to toss my trash before opening the door for me. The door-holding thing really annoyed me, but I kept my mouth shut. He had no need to court me, I didn't do long-term. And Ryan wasn't the kind of guy I'd keep even if I could. No, that would have been Gabe, but I couldn't let Gabe's sentimental crap bleed all over my night.

We walked side by side down the path, neither of us saying anything. But halfway to my dorm, he did grab my hand and lace his fingers through mine. The intimacy of the act made me push closer to him, having read him right, bumping hips. My body was waking up and thinking a little play wouldn't be so bad tonight after all. As long as he hadn't shrunk his dick, maybe he could wear me out enough to sleep for a few hours.

"You're pretty hot, Seiran Rou," Ryan said as he tugged me off the path and toward a big tree. He flipped us around so my back was to the tree and pressed up against me, all heat and man.

The flattery wasn't something I needed or enjoyed. Also, I tended to be pretty blunt. "So you know this a one-time gig, right?"

He touched my face, brushing my cheek with callused fingers. "I hear you don't let anyone double dip."

Not many even got to single dip—a hand job or a blow job were okay—but I let him kiss me anyway. He tasted of alcohol and cigarettes, neither a flavor I liked. He stepped back, smiling at me in an odd way. And then he smashed his fist into my face.

The blow knocked my head against the tree. I saw the flashing stars of consciousness trying to leak out of me as my legs gave out. I slid down the trunk of the tree. He kicked me in the stomach, doubling me up and making me heave cocoa all over. Ryan's laugh sounded far away. He began pounding me, just not the way I would have liked. My ears rung, eyesight faded in and out—probably my eyes swelling shut—but the hits kept coming to my head, stomach, arms, and hips. I rolled into a ball to protect myself.

The ground beneath me pulsed in reminder that it waited for my command. I took a moment to focus my power and breathed a calming flow of air before kicking out and nailing Ryan in the knee. I heard a satisfying pop and a cry. All I could think was "Wrong venue, asshole" as I pulled strength from the earth to help heal. The earth rolled through me, mending and giving strength but hurting and draining me as it went. It was a cycle. If I wanted the earth to help, I had to give it something in return.

Ryan leaned against a nearby tree, babying his left leg. "I'm going to fucking kill you, Rou. Fucking freak. Look what you did to me." He moved toward me, hopping and putting very little pressure on his injured leg.

I touched the ground, directing the magic toward him. A tree root broke up through the ground suddenly enough to trip him. He went sprawling, landing only a few feet from me, screaming the whole way down. I scrambled up and backed away.

"What the hell was that?" Ryan tried to get up, but his left leg was now turned at an unnatural angle. "You broke my leg."

"How did it feel to kiss a freak, asshole?" I asked him, resisting the urge to kick him in return for the beating he'd given me. "Maybe next time you'll fuck with someone who *can't* kick your ass!" It had to be the adrenaline talking, because I couldn't believe what I had said. I was so sure he'd hop up any second and beat the shit out of me. I turned and ran, heading for the dorms.

"Rou!" Ryan's voice screamed behind me. I didn't stop. My heart hammered and lungs burned. The pain pushed me to the edge of darkness several times, and only fear kept me moving. I got to the main door of the dorm and stopped to suck in deep, painful breaths. My ribs were broken for sure, at least one on each side of my chest, and flashes of pain and light kept bouncing around my head, so maybe a concussion too. If it weren't for the power of the earth coursing through me, I probably wouldn't have made it at all.

"Sei?" a soft voice whispered from a few feet away.

I staggered, trying to make out the towering figure and praying that one of Ryan's friends hadn't somehow followed me. There was probably more than one bastard out tonight.

When strong arms reached me and kept me from falling, I had to swallow the panic. The concrete beneath my feet wouldn't interfere with my magic, and I could take on anybody so long as I was in contact with the earth. But if I did something crazy, my mom would know. She'd realize I was faking not having much power. She might even kill me for using it.

"Sei? You're bleeding pretty badly, and I think you have a collapsed lung. I need to take you to the hospital." The figure sounded worried and somewhat angry; his touch was strong, but darkness ate at the edge of my vision. Something hot and annoying ran down my face. Blinking didn't help. It wasn't until the towering figure picked me up and carried me toward the parking lot that I realized it was blood on my face and Gabe carried me—I smelled his stinky shampoo.

"Gabe?" I asked.

"I got you. Let me help for once, please."

"Okay." I rested my head against his shoulder and closed my eyes, letting the pain take over as the earth recalled its power and I lost the fight against unconsciousness.

The trip to the emergency room was a first for me. I had three broken ribs, a concussion, a nasty cut on the side of my head, and a dislocated right wrist. My left lung had taken some damage, but wasn't collapsed, and so long as I breathed slow, normal breaths, it didn't ache all that much. Gabe stayed while the doctors patched me up and gave me pain meds.

A cop came by to ask about the attack and told us that Ryan had come in with a broken leg, but was claiming he'd fallen trying to get away from me. Said I tried to hex him or something, which I denied. The officer sounded angry when he talked to the doctors about me before he entered the room. I heard him grumble, "Letting a male witch enroll was just asking for trouble. Now we have one of our best offensive linemen out with a broken leg."

It wasn't until he walked in that the rage fell from his face and turned to pity. I guess a cop was a cop. I didn't need that from anyone, especially a judgmental asshole like him, so I answered his questions as quickly as I could and waited for him to leave.

When I was finally released, it was almost dawn, but Gabe was still at my side. He drove me back to the dorms and even walked me to my door inside the building. "You should go," I told him. The sun and vampires didn't mix. The fading night trickled through my window when I opened the door to my room.

"Your door has locks, right?" he asked.

"Yes. I'll be fine. Thanks."

He leaned into me, giving me a soft hug before kissing my head on the undamaged side. "I'm sorry for scaring you last night."

A hoarse laugh escaped me. He scared me? *I* scared me. I'd pulled the roots out of the ground with a thought and broke a man's leg. I hadn't been able to do that two years ago. What was wrong with me? "I'm sorry you had to rescue me."

"Not your fault. Call me, okay?"

I nodded, and he left. I watched him through the window as he headed toward his car, and prayed he would get home in time. The first edges of light were beginning to brighten the sky in the east. When he vanished from sight, I closed the door, locked it, and crawled into bed.

What a horrible night. If only I weren't a terrified idiot, I would have been at Gabe's all night. Instead I'd gotten my ass handed to me by some brainless jock, then gone to the hospital to have eleven stitches in my forehead and a million bandages. I'd seen enough of my reflection at the hospital to know my face was black and blue. How unattractive for anyone, especially someone as beautiful as Gabe.

I dozed for a few minutes before startling myself awake by thinking I heard the door. By the light coming from the window, I saw it was still locked up tight. I reached for the phone and dialed a familiar number. Gabe answered on the third ring.

"Hey. You feeling all right?" Gabe's voice was soft and sleepy. The sun always made him that way.

"Yeah. Just tired."

"Mhmm. Me too."

"How'd you find me?" It didn't worry me so much that he followed me. I didn't want to think about what might've happened if he hadn't.

"You ran into a friend of mine on campus, and he called to tell me that you looked distressed and distracted. So I drove out.

Wanted to make sure you were okay. It's my fault you were out of it."

I let that settle for a minute, trying to decide if it bothered me, but it didn't. "Can we watch a movie tonight? At your place?" Maybe cuddle on the couch in front of his theater-size TV with a bowl of popcorn and a warm protective body under a soft fleece blanket. If I'd been more awake, I might not have asked, and that would have been a tribute to the shame I already felt just for calling him. I'd need a few days to heal before I'd be up to anything strenuous again.

"Sure. Want me to pick you up after dark?"

"Yes, please."

"Okay." I could hear the smile in his voice.

"And Gabe?"

"Yeah?"

"Thanks."

"Always."

CHAPTER 1

Four Years Later.

The darkness of the forest on the new moon could have been likened to the black abyss of a cave if it weren't for the sounds of life surrounding me. Birds, bugs, a roaming raccoon—the city stretched too near for larger creatures. My power beckoned the rest, but they wouldn't come. Fear of discovery kept them at bay.

We would run together, the little things and I.

The thought eased into reality as fingers turned to clawed toes and flesh to fur. I understood the lycanthropes' draw to the full moon. They'd be home sleeping, free of the instinct on this furthest day from their change. Tonight, no one would interrupt. I'd run and chase the mice, race with the rabbits, and maybe swipe at a fox or two. This dark morning, the forest was mine.

I remembered the first change. One of the guys at military school had been a lycanthrope. I watched him shift one full moon night—horrified and fascinated by the snapping of bone and change of muscle.

A few weeks later when I tried it the first time, I expected pain. Randy always seemed to hurt when he changed. He said it got easier as he got older, but still hurt. It wasn't like that at all for me.

It was the first night of the new moon, and I wanted to be something other than myself. I even let the earth just funnel through me instead of tamping it down like I did all the time. My mom wasn't home. The house was empty, and there were acres of land in which to play.

I'd made the mistake of changing in my room with the door closed. One minute I was me with fingers and toes, and the next I had paws and fur. But I was stuck—which had been more frustrating than anything. In the end the screen of my bedroom window had paid the price for my freedom.

In the early dawn hours, I'd returned to my room, passing a mirror on the way, and only then did I realize what I was. As the years passed, the changes grew more intense—necessary, but freeing. Someday I would change and never come back, but for now I was content just to play.

I stretched in my seat, trying to keep sleep from spilling over me. Stupid 8:00 a.m. classes—they should be outlawed during the new moon.

"Seiran! Read from chapter thirty-nine." The teacher's nasal voice grated at my nerves, and her refusal to pronounce my name right just made me want to smack her. I was pretty sure she did it to irritate me.

"Yes, Professor Cokota." After a heavy sigh, I echoed the contents of the page to the room. The alignments of planets, magnetic pulls, and nature could have come from a science book rather than *The Advanced Metaphysics of Earth Magic*—a required reading.

"The new moon fuels a witch. Can anyone tell me why?" the

professor asked. Hands rose everywhere. I didn't bother. Magnetic pulls or lack thereof were common knowledge. I could have aced this class in my sleep. Why it was called Advanced Metaphysics was beyond me.

I was well aware of the pull and thought back to the previous night's adventures. They weren't allowed for non-graduates. Hell, they weren't allowed for graduates either, and certainly not for me, the only male in the class. I chuckled to myself. Nature didn't talk, and neither would I. Unfortunately I had a full class day before I'd finally be free for the weekend to consort with my wild side. If I survived the boredom.

By the time the final class ended at four thirty, I was so tired I could barely stand. Drive-thru coffee helped. Still, I dreaded having to head to the bar for the closing shift. Fortunately, the rise of the moonless night would pour more energy into my stiff muscles. Having run that morning, the pull of the earth wasn't painfully strong yet—but it would get worse as the night went on.

Smoke blanketed me through the open door to the bar. Gabe appeared by my side after I closed it. He didn't much like sunlight. It was a vampire thing.

"Can you work a double? Jo called in sick," he said. Damn, I was tired, but Friday made for good tips.

"Sure."

Gabe didn't move away. His green eyes stared at me in an appreciative sort of way.

"What?"

A tight smile crossed his lips, and pretty lips they were. "You smell like earth and power." I thought he'd say some sort of come-on, but he paused, then turned away. "Stay away from the nonhuman customers tonight. Frank will handle any lycans or vamps that come in."

With a shrug at the boss's retreating backside, which looked nice in the snug jeans he wore, I headed to the back, donned my waist apron, clad with pen and paper, and went to sling grease and beer. You couldn't get more American twenty-first century than a vampire bar with ale on tap and Angus on the fryer. The bar had gone smoke-free just two months prior, but the haze still lingered. He'd need to light the place on fire to get the stink of cigarettes out of the walls and ceilings.

"Minus all the hardware today, Say-ron?" Frank asked when I gave him a passing nod. *He* always went out of his way to pronounce my name *right*. Still it bugged me. Go figure. Mostly because I was sure Gabe had told him to or else.

Frank's baby blues looked me over like I was one of the girls he might take home later. But he was not the kind of guy who'd trade a woman for a man. Not even a girly-looking guy like me.

"Just haven't had time to put them in today." I usually had four in each ear, but had taken them out before the change last night to keep from losing them. And on new moon nights, my skin was overly sensitive and easily irritated.

I swept my long black hair up into a ponytail, pulled the rubber band off my wrist, and wrapped it around until it was tight enough to pull my hair through halfway. Keeping it up stopped people—like Frank—from tugging on it.

"Nipple rings too?"

I laughed. Was he really gonna play that game? I began to lift up my shirt. "Wanna see them up close? I bet I can rock your world like no one ever has before."

He turned and walked away, disappearing into the kitchen. His flirting was new, and since I'd called his bluff, I figured that would be the end of it for the night.

Gabe raised a brow at me from his place behind the bar. His expression asked if I was going to create a problem. But I wouldn't. Not at work, with the boss around—and he was definitely in boss mode tonight. Sigh. I guessed we were all pulling doubles today.

"Any idea what that was about?" I inquired of Gabe while I pulled up the table charts and marked my sections.

"Where are your nipple rings? That shirt hides nothing."

I gave him my sweetest smile, since he'd bought me the rings and they were the only pair I owned. "Don't worry. They're safe. I haven't lost them." My shirt was just a bar T-shirt that blazed the Bloody Bar & Grill logo in dark red on black fabric. Small hugged just right since it had been made out of that baby-soft cotton. I'd begged Gabe for that cotton on my knees more than once. He didn't like that I'd discovered he'd make a lot of promises in the throes of passion.

"Better be. Those pure white gold rings cost a fortune. And I love how it tastes on you." He teased. Snickers rose up from those closest to the bar. "Tone it down, you punks!"

Laughing my way to the first table of the night helped some of the exhaustion seep away. Not a single regular—human or otherwise—thought anything of our flirting. Gabe and I had been on-again off-again for nearly seven years. Since Matthew, he was the only guy I let have me more than once. No one else got the opportunity to get bored. Someday Gabe would, and I hoped it wouldn't hurt too much.

A handful of newbies—college boys probably thinking they'd slum tonight—looked disgusted as I approached their table. Several wouldn't look at me. The others stared with slack jaws. Was it the hip-high lace-up boots, the tight black jeans, or the snug T-shirt? Was it the incident with Frank? Either way, they looked at me like I was one of those cleavage-rich, Hooters girls who'd just offered the ugly guy a lap dance.

Oh, this would be fun.

I pulled up a chair, reversed it, and sat down, making them inch away. "Evening, boys, my name's Seiran. Welcome to the Bloody Bar. First time? I'll make sure it's sweet and gentle all the way through. Or maybe you'd like it a little rough and raw?

Either way I'm sure you'll leave with a *sweet* memory of the juicy meat you indulged in here."

More than one face turned red.

"So what can I start you with? A pitcher or two of beer? Some chips, maybe?" I spread my legs out, stretching them long, and pressed my hips to the chair rungs, proving I was all boy. As soon as I was sure they'd noted the fact, I leaned on my hand, giving them my most innocent expression.

The one closest to me, who had metrosexual, spiky light brown hair, gulped and said, "A couple of pitchers please, and chips would be great." He looked me over like a many a straight boy in search of a secret indulgence did.

I threw him a smile and got up, putting the chair back at a nearby table. "Be right back with that. Browse the menu while I'm gone. The burgers on page three are a real cherry-popping experience. And the special sauce will make you *cream* with pleasure."

They all flipped through their menus as I walked back to the bar to request the pitchers. Gabe just shook his head at me. "Leave it to you to make a bunch of homophobic jocks drool."

"Are they drooling already? I haven't even started yet." A bowl of chips and salsa appeared from the kitchen on the serving counter. A glance up told me half the boys' eyes were still on me. I threw them another smile. All heads ducked back down to their menu.

"Those boys best have brought money. Your smiles aren't cheap," Jack, one of our regulars, said from his seat at the bar.

I flashed him a grin on my way to deliver beer and chips. "Always a free one for you, Jackie."

After dropping off the starters and taking their orders, I got pretty busy. A whirl of both human and nonhuman customers kept the tables flying. Frank sneered when one of my lycan friends came in to ask for me. Since he was a lycan, I wasn't allowed to play bar whore for him—which usually meant sitting on his lap and making all his friends jealous. Those sorts of things got me great tips. Apparently tonight was going to be a lackluster night all around. Still, he'd stopped me briefly to ask if I wanted to meet up after work. Because it was the new moon, I declined. I'd have liked to run and fuck. But Gabe was right about how my powers affected others during the absence of the moon. It scared me how much he knew about me sometimes. More at how much he was right.

Midway through the night, a group of vampires I didn't recognize came in. Gabe seated them in the back away from all my tables. Frank just gave me a dirty look when I asked who they were. I knew most of the vampires in the cities because they all visited Gabe—and the bar—often.

The jocks at table four stuck around. They'd eaten dinner and still munched on chips and drank beer. The one with the light brown hair was starting to get loud. I was pretty sure at least one of them had a fake ID, but had no way to prove it. Fortunately, they'd already paid their bill, and Gabe had sent them their last pitcher, effectively cutting them off.

I piled up a bunch of dirty dishes from other tables and dropped them off by the kitchen sink. By the time I returned to the dining area, Brown Hair was on his feet, hand on the arm of one of the duo of ladies that came to the bar regularly. Her partner was pitching a fit in a shrieky girl voice that hurt my ears.

Gabe raised a brow in my direction, asking with that one look if I needed help. I just shook my head in reply—I could handle one little jock trying to pick a fight with a couple of girls—and stepped up to the jock's side. My hand on his bicep made him turn. He looked ready to take a swing at me, but I gave him that hundred-watt smile again. He dropped Betsy's arm.

"Lara, take Betsy to the bar for a drink. On me." As they walked away, I asked the jock, "You wouldn't want to make Betsy upset, right, *friend*?"

"Brock. My name is Brock."

"Brock. That's a very athletic type of name. Are you and your buddies ready to go?"

Brock looked like he wanted to say something, but one of his friends, this one blond and familiar looking, pulled him away as the other guys got up and prepared to leave. As I waited for them to gather their things, I felt someone's eyes on me. Who else was looking for a fight?

I scanned the room quickly and found Frank glaring at me for a few more seconds before his attention flipped to someone behind me. I turned and followed his gaze to the corner, where Gabe now stood with his back to me. He was speaking to a man with dark hair and bright blue eyes. Another vampire, who was staring at me as if he knew me.

"Seiran?" It was Brock again. Hadn't they left yet?

Had I seen that vampire before? He didn't look like my type, but I was known for being a little on the loose side with one-night stands. "Yes, Brock?" My attention swung back to the annoying jock beside me, and I tried to ignore the vampire.

"Nice to meet you," he said before he was dragged out the door by his friends. The rabble finally gone, I cleaned up their table, happy for the twenty they'd left me as a tip. That at least made the trouble worthwhile.

"I don't know how you pull that shit off," Frank said as he passed me on the way to the kitchen. "Anyone else would be arrested for harassment."

"You're just jealous, Frankie."

"Yep, if I had half of what you got, I'd have a bed full of chicks waiting for me at home. Why you choose dick over that, I dunno."

The disgust in his voice made me laugh as I took the order from another table. Frankie, the vampire wannabe, couldn't rile me if he tried. He retreated to another table of lycans, and I shrugged at him, smile firmly in place. I never knew if he really hated gays—which seemed odd since he worshiped Gabe, and being bi made Gabe as good as gay in any homophobe's book—or if it was because I was a male witch who got a lot of attention.

I peeked in the direction of the unfamiliar vampire again. Mysterious Blue Eyes still stood there. His eyes locked with mine the second he saw me, and uneasiness settled in the pit of my belly. Who was this guy? Seconds passed before I could look away.

"Seiran," Gabe said, stepping between me and the new vamp. He took a firm grip on my arm and led me to the kitchen. "Please see to your customers."

It was unlike him to be so cold; it stung a little. "Sorry," I muttered, though I didn't know what I did wrong. How long *had* I been standing there staring? "Friend of yours visiting?" I nodded to the vampire in the corner.

He stopped, face stern, body tense. "I have no friends." He stepped closer and whispered, "Neither do you. Get back to work." Then he disappeared back behind the bar.

I brushed off his cold demeanor, reminding myself we weren't a couple. Gabe and I had history, and sure, he had snapped at me a time or two. It wasn't anything I couldn't deal with. I recognized boss mode when I saw it and knew he had to play tough at work. I tried not to let it bother me.

A new rush of customers began to pour into the bar, which meant a baseball game must have let out. Being at the edge of downtown Minneapolis, we had several venues nearby—Target Field and the Target Center were the big two—that usually kept us hopping. The TVs blared several different sports channels, and I could never keep up. Were the Twins playing or a college game, I wondered, but went back to work, flirting and serving to the best of my ability while ignoring the probing eyes from the corner.

Gabe shrugged off more than a handful of busty admirers. I wasn't jealous, couldn't be. Occasional casual sex didn't make us lovers. Declaring him one would have lessened my tips, since many liked to think they stood a chance with me. No one needed to know I was a lot pickier than I used to be and rarely chose someone from the bar.

Jamie, Gabe's usual barman, showed up late. He helped me with the crowd and warned strange men away from me with a look that signaled angry boyfriend, though we'd never been lovers. Not that he wasn't attractive.

"It's not them, it's you," Jamie said snidely as I growled at the measly two-dollar tip left at the table of guys he'd just ushered out after they offered to buy me a drink.

"Is there some reason you have to be such an ass? You're killing my tips." I stuffed the money in my apron pocket and let my hair down, willing to take whatever just to bring in the dough. Being small and cute helped. Drunk guys couldn't often tell if I was a boy or a girl with my hair down, so they got lewd and loud, but almost always tipped well.

"Because I'm good at it?" Jamie gave me his odd, lopsided smile and swept his long blond hair over his shoulder. Very Fabio-like. He needed the ponytail holder more than I did. Mine was just long; his was thick too. But the girls had been all over him tonight. He probably had his rubber band wrapped around the large wad of cash tips stuffed in his pants. No man had a package that big.

"Apparently. But I'd appreciate it if you didn't scare off my clients."

"Clients? I didn't know you were taking payment for your after-work services now."

Okay, that was low. "You son of a—!"

"Seiran, table five needs to be cleared," Gabe said as he passed with a plate of food and a pitcher of beer. "Jamie, back to work. I don't pay you to chat with employees."

Jamie grumbled his way back to the bar, his tight butt in snug leather gaining nearly as many stares as Gabe did in his jeans. I cleared table five and flirted with an African-American man and his wife at table three. They gave me a ten-dollar tip.

I caught an irritated look from Jamie as I put away the couple's credit card slip. What was his problem? He looked like he'd swallowed a live fish and it was trying to wriggle its way back up. I shook my head and continued on like it didn't matter, pulling up a pitcher and filling it for one of my tables.

"You shouldn't do that," Jamie said.

My eyes shifted from the pitcher filling with golden brew to Jamie and then back again. "Huh?"

"Let those men degrade you. They slobber all over you like you're some kind of stripper. You're not even a girl, but they all do it anyway. Why do you let them?"

I swallowed a laugh, set the beer on the counter, put my foot up on the shelf behind the bar, and pressed my inner thigh against him. There'd be no mistaking that I was a guy. What was his deal, anyway? Jealous, maybe? "Why haven't you and I fucked before? I prefer to bottom, but I can top if you swing that way." I gave him my million-watt smile. "You're stacked, and I can get you ready in no time. Maybe we can hit the bathroom for a quick break? Bet I can suck you off before Gabe even notices were missing."

His horrified expression made me wonder if I'd been wrong about him. Gabe came out of the kitchen and gave me a glare angry enough to make anyone shudder. I put my leg down and headed back to my tables.

Later Gabe stopped me, his grip a little rougher than usual. "Leave Jamie alone."

"Is he a reformed homosexual or something? What the hell?" I tried to read his expression, but it was neutral. Something was off about him tonight.

"If I say yes, will you let it go?"

I shook off his grip and rubbed my wrist. There'd be a bruise there tomorrow. "Maybe."

"Then let me put it this way. If you fuck him, you're fired. If you blow him, you're fired. You do anything with him that can be considered sex in any country, by any religion, and you're fired. Got it?"

The counter behind me stopped me from backing away from him, but I could finally see the heat of his anger on his face. "Oh no. You don't get to decide who I do and don't sleep with. We aren't a couple, Gabe."

He shook his head at me. "He's not your type. Don't torment him. I know how you get when you have your eye on someone."

Why was he so angry? What did I do that I didn't always do? This wasn't like Gabe. "Not my type? What the hell does that mean?"

Everyone's eyes were on us. Gabe gestured me to the back door. I sighed and stomped ahead of him. When he shut the door and the cold air of the night settled around me, I shivered. "What the hell is your problem tonight?"

"You're a player, Seiran. You see every man as a conquest. Do you care for anyone?" He sounded tired, worn down. He was tired of me. That's what he had to be saying. I guess it had to end sometime.

"That's a shitty thing for you to ask, since you and I have a date tomorrow."

"It's not a date. You and I get together and have sex. There's no romance. You hate romance unless it's in one of those books you read. I'm pretty sure you wouldn't know love if it slapped you in the face." His voice went low and rough. He turned away so I couldn't see his expression anymore. What was he hiding from me?

I gave him back the anger he threw at me. "You've been around a couple thousand years, Gabe. How much do you believe in love anymore? And what's wrong with sex? If you don't want me, then so be it. But don't tell me who I can and can't have sex with. Is Jamie your new love toy? How long before he bores you too?"

He threw his hands up in the air as if in defeat. "That's exactly it! Always my fault. You're flying high as a kite tonight with all that new moon power riding you, swinging into people's laps and touching them inappropriately 'cause you don't have a care in the world, and somehow it's my fault you're being an ass. Leave Jamie alone. That's my last warning. Now get back to work." He stomped inside, letting the door slam behind him.

When I got back inside, the place seemed quieter, like they were all staring at me and amused by the soap opera that made up my life. Jamie's chocolate-brown eyes looked sad. They flicked from me to Gabe and back again. He stood behind the bar, passing out drinks, but not smiling. Did he know he was part of the rift?

The pretty dark-haired vamp with blue eyes sat in his booth, looking interested. I didn't even try to smile at him. My drama, his soap opera. Bastard.

Gabe's angry words ate at me while the rest of the night flew by. I let my irritation build and remembered instances such as this were the reason why I didn't do relationships. My first lover —Matthew—had taught me that time only makes the relationship grow dull. And if what I offered wasn't enough for Gabe anymore, so be it. I could handle it. Maybe, probably. I sighed. In fact, I couldn't stop the sighs, rising from me several times before we closed. Thankfully, we were sweeping, cleaning off tables, and putting up chairs before it seemed possible that the night was almost over.

Frank licked his lips and bumped me hard enough to nearly knock me over. "You looking to take someone home tonight?"

"Not you. He doesn't want fleas," Jamie said as he walked by carrying the last stack of dishes to the washer.

I shuddered at the thought. "You don't even do boys, Frankie."

"Not Jamie either," Gabe said, his calm voice back in place. Was he still mad at me? Was I still mad at him? I sighed again.

Both Frank and I turned to look at Gabe, who seemed momentarily confused. Then his cheeks reddened. He must have had a bottle or two of QuickLife in the back. Frank's spine stiffened, and he huffed his way to the kitchen.

Jamie reappeared. "What'd I miss?"

"Gabe's fucking me tonight."

Jamie paused but then just shrugged and said, "Okay." I guess if they had a relationship, Gabe was the only possessive one in it, which made no sense to me.

Mr. Blue Eyes had left only a half an hour before, and something about the visit seemed to bother Gabe. Maybe he wanted to talk about it, but I was still pissed and not really feeling up to another lecture. I'd prodded Jamie and Frank for info but only been shrugged off. Maybe another time I'd have pushed harder, but anger made everyone do stupid things.

Once everyone was shooed out and everything clean, we all headed for the door. I stripped out of the apron, waiting for him to let us out. Gabe—still in boss mode—lifted a brow in my direction, checking to see if I wanted to go home with him. I shook my head at him, signaling I wasn't on board, not yet willing to put the anger at his attitude aside.

He walked me to my car. "You sure you don't want to come home with me?"

"Maybe another time." I gave him the brush-off, at least until I could sort through my irritation at him.

He gifted me with a tight smile, hovering close enough to nearly be attached to my side. "I'm sorry if I was harsh with you earlier. I was in a bad headspace. Sometimes I just wish you'd commit...."

I kissed him, forcing my tongue in to taste his, and to get him to shut up. He returned the kiss. When I pulled away, I said, "It's better this way. I'm high maintenance, complicated, and terrified of commitment. You don't need any of that."

"Seiran…."

"Good night, Gabe."

"Don't forget we have a date tonight."

I nodded since I hadn't forgotten. At least I didn't have to work. I got in my clunker and headed for the flat I called home. The rest of the weekend was mine. I glanced up at the dark sky. Two more nights to play in the moonlessness. The sprawling, wild land to the south of the city throbbed in my bones. Soon, I promised myself. Sleep first. Magic later.

CHAPTER 2

A couple of hours of uninterrupted sleep worked wonders. A shower to wash away the previous night's bar smoke was bliss. The clock ticked past noon before I stepped out, wrapped myself in a towel, and relaxed on the couch to comb the wet tangles from my hair.

In less than eight hours, the sun would set.

The moon throbbed invisibly in the sky, calling to my magic. The gloominess of the fall had set in though it was barely September, predicting cold rain. Maybe no one would be in the forest. I'd probably still need Gabe later, but for now I had to stretch my muscles and run. I dressed in sweats and headed for the door, never expecting to find Frank on my doorstep.

Dead.

Obviously, he'd been gone a while.

His head was turned almost all the way around. Blood stained the corner of his lips. His legs were bent at angles that defied human anatomy, and a rib or two protruded from his chest. He just looked broken.

The next few hours passed in a blur. I barely remember the

lady across the hall coming out and screaming before slamming her door shut. The police, however, were more than thrilled to talk to me. They kept asking me the same questions over and over.

"Maybe you should come down to the station," the older cop said. His name had been Reith or something along that line.

"Do I need a lawyer?" I blinked at him, more than a little disoriented from the power that was pulling at me but being denied. How many years had it been since I'd missed changing on a new moon night? Too many to count for sure.

"Do you?"

"Do I get a free one?"

"Only if you admit to killing him."

I glanced at the body bag and its very lumpy outline and shook my head. "How exactly did I do that? I'm five four and a buck thirty. Frank was six two and well over two hundred pounds. I'm a magic studies major, not physics, but pretty sure that doesn't work out as probable."

"You're a witch, right? A male witch." He sounded incredulous.

"My mom is part of the Dominion. It sort of runs in the family." Something that pissed her off every time she saw me. Mostly because I was male and went out of my way to act anything but in her presence. If she hadn't been telling me she'd wanted a daughter instead of a son for the past twenty-two years, I might have turned out differently.

"Were you and Frank seeing one another?" the other cop asked. He was young, the smiling sort, ordinary brown eyes and dark hair. Who was Good Cop and who was Bad Cop? So far being questioned wasn't much like the movies.

"We worked together at the same bar."

"Bloody Bar & Grill. A vampire bar."

"There's only one vampire there, but he owns it, so yeah, I guess you could call it a vampire bar." The afternoon light began to fade. Had it been that long already? My skin itched with the need to be outside.

"When was the last time you saw him?" Reith asked. He had that sort of hard-nosed cop face that made people want to start confessing just to make him stop staring.

"Gabe, or Frank, the dead guy?"

Reith gave me a look that said he didn't appreciate my smartass attitude. "The dead guy."

"At 3:00 a.m. when we closed the bar."

"And where was your vampire friend?"

"He walked me to my car. Frank had already driven off."

"And you have no idea what Mr. Sither was doing, dead, on your doorstep?"

"No. Not like I could ask him, could I?"

"Did you hear anything? A knock, any sort of struggle?" the young cop asked.

"No, but I slept late, then got in the shower." This wasn't nearly as fun as TV made it out to be. Where were the hot cops in nice clothes to analyze the killer's thoughts and puzzle it out in sexy ways?

The crowd of coppies filling the hallway thinned, and a tall man with dark hair and pretty blue eyes stepped up. He wasn't the kind of handsome man I'd been hoping for. I had to glance back inside to see out the window, but sure enough, the sun was still up, and yet the strange vampire from the bar was there. He smiled at me again, like he knew me.

"Seiran Rou?" His accent held a bit of southern twang. I wondered briefly what had brought him to the frozen tundra of Minnesota. "I'm Detective Andrew Roman. Can I come in? Maybe we can sit down and I can ask you a few questions?"

"I don't invite vampires into my home. But you can ask me what you need."

"Does Gabe Santini have an invite?"

"No. And I don't see what that has to do with anything." Not at the moment he didn't. I often revoked his invite whenever he irritated me.

Roman's smile didn't dim at all. "You're studying Earth Magic at the U of M, right?"

"Yes."

"What does your mother think of that?"

I snorted. "Does that matter?"

"Tanaka Rou is a well-known member of the Dominion. This could be an attack on her. Set you up for murder, ruin her name...."

"My mother would tell you that I ruin her name with my very existence. Now, are you going to arrest me or not? Because I'd really like to go for a run now." I pulled my hair up into a loose ponytail, grabbed the bag full of clothes that had already been searched four times, and stepped around the detective.

He handed me his card. "If you remember anything or see anything unusual, call me."

"Sure, sure." I headed out the door, to my car, and across town, convinced they were following me. So much for being able to run for the day. They'd arrest me for sure if they saw me change. My mother would be thrilled to lead the execution for unlawful use of earth magic. She was just waiting for an excuse.

Gabe's apartment in the city was nice. He lived in one of those St. Paul high-rises that probably cost a fortune. It had an open loft sort of feel, with walls of windows, which was odd for a vampire, them not liking sunlight and all.

He wasn't home when I let myself in, and I knew from experience that wherever he rested during the day was nearby, but outside the apartment. He always came through the front door.

Thankfully, the sun would set early tonight. I could wait, bleed off some energy. The new moon pulled at me, but there were other ways to use that energy, and right now I needed some physical comfort.

Gabe kept everything so immaculately clean. I wondered

where the neat freak in him had come from. The wood floors gleamed, bed was made army-style, and windows were so clear they were nonexistent.

I rearranged the magazines on his coffee table in alphabetical order. It really wasn't much more than a show room. Gabe didn't really live here. He didn't live anywhere. He said *I* had commitment issues, but he couldn't even stay in one place for long.

The fall of the darkness quickened my heart. I chose my position, my attire—or lack thereof—and my gift wisely: a warmed bottle of QuickLife in hand, O positive, Gabe's favorite. The leather armchair moved ten feet from the door. Lube resting on the table beside me. Hip-length boots, one leg up on the arm of the chair and the other curled over the opposite arm. I was ready when the doorknob turned. Anticipation made me hard, and the white gold of the nipple rings flashed in my reflection from the windows as I stroked myself with my free hand.

He froze in the doorway, dark eyes focused exactly where I wanted them to be. The door closed, and his hands ran up my legs before I'd even realized he'd crossed the room. Exuberant, probably because I'd denied him this morning. He nuzzled my balls before taking the bottle from my grasp.

I didn't watch him drink, because it was like a good beer, he'd savor it for a moment or two. I picked up the bottle of lube and flipped the cap open.

"Ready when you are."

"You're pure evil," he mumbled. The bottle of QuickLife clanged into the trash nearby. His dark eyes held a tinge of red. He hadn't had enough to turn them human in appearance. He knelt between my legs, bringing his mouth to that aching hole I so wanted him to fill.

"Please, Gabe."

He pulled me forward for a heated kiss. I thought for sure he'd unbutton his tight jeans and fill me, but then he was gone, up and moving away toward the bedroom, stripping off his gray tank top and pulling a fresh shirt out of the closet.

What the hell? I followed him, boots clapping on the wood. He loved these boots. And he'd never turned me down before when I wore them.

"Frank's dead, and you just wanna fuck," he said.

"I want you to fuck me, yes. What does Frank have to do with anything?"

Gabe looked pissed. "I'm going to work. I've got no one else to cover the bar."

"Jo and Jamie can handle it."

"Jo asked for an extended leave. I said yes."

I blinked. She was the only witch I liked. And she'd worked for Gabe longer than me. "Say what?"

"She was sleeping with Frank."

"So? I'd like to sleep with you."

He turned his back to me. "No, you wouldn't. I sleep in dirt. Face to a concrete block. You're far too prissy for that."

I crawled on the bed beside him and let bare skin and the black leather boots do a little peekaboo show. "Just a quickie? Please?"

"You're heartless."

"Says the vampire who won't comfort the guy who found a dead coworker on his doorstep. I thought the cops were going to arrest me."

"I'm also the vampire who's gotta go run a bar by himself because his Manager on Duty was murdered, and that M.O.D.'s girl tried to quit to mourn her boy toy's death. Get a grip, Sei. You're on a power high. In two days you'll be angry at me for letting all this go and doing you instead. Jamie needs a babysitter. I can't imagine what he'd do to my bar on his own."

I sank down on the corner of the bed, hard-on wilting from lack of attention. The second he turned my way, I gave him a heated kiss that begged for everything he'd been denying. "Fuck me. Please."

He shook his head. "Next month, Seiran. When the new moon rises, I'll give you the whole week off. We'll find some new workers, and you and me, we'll go somewhere. Just you and me and no moon to fuck up the energy between us."

It sounded sweet, but unlikely. "Can't we just have a quickie? Then you can go to work?"

He yanked a T-shirt out of the closet and threw it at me. "Get dressed."

Reluctantly, I put the shirt on. "Can we meet later? After you close the bar?" I begged. I could run for a few hours. Get lost in the feeling. Hopefully, I could shake the cops that were probably following me.

He threw me my pair of sweats. I'd left them in his closet when getting ready for him to arrive. "I need you to work tonight. Come out of the clouds for me."

"Wrong kinda witch."

He threw his hands up in frustration. "Fine. Get your head out of the sand or out of your ass. Whatever way it has sunk. I've got a business to run and a funeral to plan."

"Jo can do that."

"He was my servant. I owe him."

"He was a jerk who probably got caught by something bigger and badder than him. Why was he flirting with me last night? That was so out of character. Maybe he hit on some bar brawler and got the wrong end of a baseball bat."

"He was just doing what you always do."

Point. I pulled on the sweats, not really liking how they felt over the boots. But unlacing the boots took forever without help. The feel of his stare made me look up. "What?"

"I need you to be smart and not let this power high throw you for a loop. I know you act this way to piss off your mom, but I really need the adult Seiran tonight."

Again with the work. I followed him to his car, which was parked in the outside lot. "I don't have anything other than sweats and the boots with me."

"Wear the sweats. You have enough people slobbering all over you anyway."

I shrugged. "Better tips."

"I pay you well. If you gave up your apartment, you'd have more money. The loft is paid for."

And lonely when the sun came up. "Are you offering to be my sugar daddy?"

"Would you accept the offer if I did? If I said this thing with Frank may be trouble and you'd be safer, would you come live with me?"

I shook my head. "You'd get bored having me around all the time, eventually."

"Was it your mom who made you this cynical?"

"You have a fetish with my mom?"

He put the key in the ignition, turned, and kissed me softly. Since I was in the mood for hard and fast, it didn't do much to quell the growing desire. "I'm crazy about you," he said when I didn't respond with my usual fervor. "Every fucked-up bit of you."

"Ha." I pulled away to stare out the window, feeling uncomfortable in my skin. Only Gabe could do that. "The packaging is false advertising. Don't get caught up."

"No shit." Gabe started the car. We didn't talk the whole way across town. Traffic was heavy, as always on Saturday nights. My skin crawled with the need to shift. But I'd caught more than one glimpse of a tailing car. "Let's hope it's the cops," Gabe said, like he could read my thoughts. "If you *do* shift, go up to Jay Cooke State Park. It's farther to drive, but easier for you to lose them in."

"I can't change if I gotta work. And you won't even fuck me to bleed off the energy."

There was only one car in the parking lot of the bar. Jamie

leaned against it, looking tired and worried. Some of the tension in his shoulders eased when we got out. Was he worried something had happened to Gabe?

"Hello, Seiran. Nice outfit."

"Don't tempt him. There's nothing under those pants but black boots." Gabe walked past him to the door.

If I hadn't been on such an earth high, I might have had a nasty retort. Right at this moment, Jamie just looked really good. Blond hair trailed over his shoulders, wet from a shower, probably. A snug black sweater fitted over a nicely muscled chest. He had a workout fetish. Sometimes he stank of sweat when he came into the bar. My bitching had made him shower more, at least when he knew I was on duty. But maybe Gabe had said something too. Thankfully, he smelled like earth and man tonight. That's all that really mattered. The tan pants that clung to his hips, outlining his way-too-large-to-be-real package, made me lick my lips.

"Seiran!"

I blinked at the sound of Gabe's voice, realizing I was suddenly very close to a concerned-looking Jamie.

"I already warned you once."

"But you won't play." My voice sounded weak, more like a half-whispered complaint.

Gabe grabbed my arm and dragged me along with him.

Jamie followed us inside. "You should just close for the night. One night won't kill your revenue."

"You know nothing about my revenue."

"I know a lot more than you think. You shouldn't have brought him here. He needs to be outside. The wards only do so much."

Gabe let me go, shoved me toward the bar, and growled at Jamie. "My office, Browan. Now."

"What? Can't talk about me with me here?" I demanded. My hands itched with the need to shift. Maybe if I just went all kitty on him he'd ease up. Gabe set a large glass of beer down in front of me before heading to his office, Jamie in tow. They closed the door. Bastards.

I took a sip of the beer, but it tasted like minerals. All things did at that time of the month. Damn. I spit it out and poured the rest down the sink. A vent opening to the upper left side of the bar gave me an idea. The cover came off with patience and slow movement to keep it from clanking. I yanked off my clothes in a hurry and let the power of the earth absent the moon flow into my veins and let the change come. Less than a minute later I shook out my fur and leapt from the floor to the counter to the open vent. Thankfully, since my change was all magic my size was that of a normal lynx and not some man-sized mockery of one. Otherwise I would not have fit in the tiny opening and ductwork.

"I don't see the connection. Roman's been here for years," Jamie was saying as I arrived at the other side.

"It's obvious. The papers have been merciless." Gabe was pacing, something I'd only seen him do once or twice before. "Any other reason Frank might be dead?" He glared pointedly at Jamie.

"You think I did it?"

Gabe's raised brow asked the question. "Frank was hitting on Sei last night. I know how much anyone flirting with him irritates you."

"I don't know what Frank's deal was last night, but he wouldn't have dared. Not with your claim. Besides, if it'd been me, you'd have never found the body. I certainly wouldn't have left it on Seiran's doorstep. It sounds more like something his mother would do."

The thought made me shudder, which resounded like a loud thump in the vent. Turning to dash away, I prayed I'd get enough of a chance to break free of the metal cave and scurry away to avoid Gabe's wrath. However, he waited for me on the other side. Damn vampire speed.

He bravely held out his arms. "Come here, Sei."

I backed farther into the vent, cursing the dust bunnies that clung to my fur. I'd so need another shower. Jamie's smell came from the other side of the tunnel, like he was waiting for me to try going that way.

"*Come here.*" This time the tone was undeniable. And it made me angry as my body moved without my consent. Leaping into his arms, I turned out my claws at that last moment, digging in deep. He grunted in reply.

Jamie stepped out of the office. "Got him?"

Had me, he did. Gabe's grip hurt probably as much as my claws in his arms and shoulders did. "Stop fighting me, and I'll let you change back." Gabe dropped me to the floor. "Don't spy on me."

I took a heavy swipe at Jamie, who held out his hands like he was innocent, before disappearing behind the bar to change back. The fur receded like water into my skin, smooth, easy, and pain-less because of the new moon. I pulled on the borrowed clothes before rising from my hiding place. The shirt and sweats were rough against my skin. The boots would not be going back on tonight. I raised a fist to punch Gabe for his trouble.

"Do it and I'll fire you."

"Fire me! Do it! How dare you command me?" I'd given him blood more than once. We both knew that gave him power over me. Especially when my brain was simplified in lynx form. He'd promised to never use it. "You—!" I couldn't even think of what terrible things I wanted to call him. The change still rode me. It hadn't been enough to slip my skin. I needed to run. The earth was calling me.

"You should just go home," he finally said.

"You're the one who dragged me here."

Gabe snapped up a newspaper off the counter and shoved it

into my face. The cover read "Another Vampire Pal Dead, Sixth Serial Slaying." However, the article wasn't about Frank. His death was too new to have made the paper today. "People are dying just for being seen with vampires. Frank was probably killed by this psycho and then left as warning for you."

"I'm a witch, not a vampire."

"But they know you're fucking a vampire."

"Not tonight. You had your chance." I stalked toward the door, throwing my boots over my shoulder. The gravel parking lot was going to hurt.

"Seiran, you really should take this seriously." Jamie matched my step.

I shrugged. No one had ever really cared much about what happened to me. Why start now? "My apartment is warded."

"Jamie, take him home."

Jamie and I looked at each other, both a little stunned.

Gabe wanted us alone together?

"So help me, Sei, if you try to seduce him again, I'll save the serial killer the trouble."

Escape was good. Something more than Frank's death was bothering him. Maybe I could get some answers from Jamie. I picked my way slowly to Jamie's car. Jamie thankfully said nothing until we were headed away from the bar. Then we both spoke at once.

"He's been on edge."

"He's a bit cranky." We sat in silence a moment longer, then I said, "Let's not go home."

Jamie frowned. "I am not doing anything with you, Seiran."

"Why? Because Gabe has some sort of claim on me? He doesn't own me. We aren't dating. Just casual lovers."

"Vamps don't do anything casual. And don't talk out loud about not being his. He's not the only big vamp in the city. They'd all like a chance to control a power like yours."

"I'm a guy. My power means nothing in witch standards."

"A guy with more power than ninety percent of the Dominion. If your mom knew what you could really do—"

"She'd kill me."

Jamie eased on to the highway, headed far away from town. Thankfully there were no headlights behind us. Maybe we'd finally shaken the tail the police had on us. "She's a really evil woman."

"She's my mom." I stared out the window. "So who's Andrew Roman? What's he mean to Gabe?"

"Other than a cop, you mean?"

"You know what I mean."

"They're both from the same time. Roman's got secrets, though. Don't trust him. The badge is just the means to an end." Jamie slid the car to a stop near the forest where I usually ran, Nerstrand Big Woods. Had he guessed, or did he somehow know? "Gabe just wants to keep you safe."

The thought made me a little tense. I knew Gabe worried a lot. It was just the sort of guy he was. I just didn't want to be a burden to him, or anyone, really.

I got out, the night pouring over me. Earth calling me home so strongly, I just needed to run. "The cops may have followed us."

Jamie shook his head as he got out of the car. When he stepped around the metal, I felt it. A surge of power from the earth. The strong bursts of wind around us whistled through the trees, and the peace of home settle over me.

I'd worked with him for months and never had a clue. "You're a witch too? Earth, like me. How did I not know this?"

His lopsided smile returned before he gestured to the open forest. "Going to run before the rain? Or perhaps you're afraid you'll get wet? Being a kitten and all."

I wanted to ask what the hell he was, but it didn't matter at this point. I stripped out of my borrowed clothes and changed with a surge from the welcoming earth. Paws to the ground, I was energized, powerful, peaceful, *free*. Jamie looked huge. I watched him change into a large brown grizzly bear. Not native to the area, but he had plenty of room to run too.

Shit, he was huge.

He wavered slightly on his hind legs, arms in the air, before lumbering toward me. I turned and ran, knowing I could outrun him. He had bigger claws, but I was faster, lighter, and more cunning in my attacks. This would be fun.

I climbed a nearby tree with little effort, watching as the bear dropped to all fours and followed. He stood at the bottom of the tree reaching for me, but I was too far up.

An owl hooted and I jumped from my branch to the next tree, searching for it. The bear grunted below me as I moved through the trees, rousing squirrels and chipmunks, darting up and down the trunks. There was a tree full of little worker ants that I watched for a time. They marched right by me unbothered, carrying things I couldn't recall the names for—other bugs maybe?

The bear grunted below me. Was he mad I wasn't playing? Well he was sort of in my territory anyway. I leapt down, landing right in front of him and swiped at his nose with one of my giant paws. He rose up onto his back legs, towering over me while I arched my back and growled.

Before he could take a step in my direction, I jumped to another tree trunk, dug my claws in deep, and found my way above him again. He fell back to all fours and seemed to huff in frustration. Bears couldn't climb trees, at least not big bears. I'd seen baby bears do it a time or two, but was pretty sure I was safe in the multicolored swatches of leaves.

He wandered away, sniffing the ground and pawing through piles of roughage. Probably for food—which reminded me that I was hungry. I caught the scent of mice and followed their trail until I caught one tiny squeaking critter under a paw. Just as I bent to bite and end the little mouse's life for a tasty treat, the bear landed behind me heavily enough to shake the trees.

The mouse escaped. I watched him run into the hollow of a tree knowing it was too small a hole to follow him through. He'd been a chubby mouse, ready for winter, and would have made a good snack. I glared at the bear.

The bear sniffed me—tongue coming out to lick my face. Gross! I leapt backward back into the tree and hissed at him from above. He sat on his back legs, swaying slightly and staring up into the branches like he couldn't quite see me.

After another few minutes and a stiff blowing of a cold wind, he wandered away again. This time I followed from above. He used the trunk of a tree to scratch his back and dug in more than one bush—even the thorny ones I usually avoided.

In the distance I felt the prickling of the sun. Had time gone by so quickly? I watched the bear a moment longer, timing it just right as I jumped out of the tree and landed claws first in the bear's back—a little thank-you present for losing me my dinner. I darted away in happy triumph when he howled and shook. My claws couldn't do much to him anyway. But it did send him running after me. And that was okay, there was a little more time before the sun was to rise.

CHAPTER 3

W hen I woke up in a strange apartment, I had that instant brain panic of *Oh, shit, what did I do?* The bed smelled like Jamie—and not in a good way, but thankfully he wasn't in it with me. I rolled out and looked around the room. I still had my sweats and T-shirt. That was a good sign. The sound of water running came from a doorway to the right. The bathroom? The water turned off, and a few seconds later, Jamie stepped out, swabbing his hair with a towel, another wrapped around his hips.

"Glad you're awake," he said as he walked past me to the dresser. "Shower's free."

I hurried past him into the bathroom, glad that my morning wood hadn't lasted beyond smelling the dirty sheets of Jamie's bed. Had we done something? Gabe was going to be so mad. Last thing I remembered was jumping out of a tree and landing on the big bear's back. Holy crap, Jamie was a witch like me! Did Gabe know?

The shower didn't help wash away the confusion. Would Jamie notice if I cleaned his bathroom? I found a spray under the sink and did a quick once-over of the stall before leaving the bathroom. A stack of clothes which all appeared new and my size sat on Jamie's bed.

"Are you some kind of stalker?" I asked him as I pulled a T-shirt over my head and hopped into a pair of faded blue jeans.

"Why would you say that?" Jamie pulled out two coffee mugs, poured one black and the other with three sugars and a bunch of cream, just how I liked it.

"Uh, because you knew where I usually go to run. You know my sizes and now how I take my coffee." Oh yeah, he was a stalker. I so needed to go home. No wonder Gabe wanted me to stay away.

"I'm an observant guy."

"Creepy." I sighed, took a sip of the coffee, because it was good and deserved a bit of revering, then blurted out, "Did we fuck last night? Because I don't remember, and I really don't want to get fired for something I don't remember."

He folded his big arms across his chest and shook his head at me, like an adult humoring a child. "No. I don't like you that way. You were so tired in the car I brought you here. And with the Frank thing, I thought this would be safer." *This* meaning the disaster that was his apartment. It looked okay on the outside, or if you didn't stare too long and see the piles of dust in the corner or the grime in the sink, or realize how badly the sheets smelled.

"Good. Great. Can you take me home?"

"It's safer here."

I put the coffee cup down and headed for the door, wishing I'd had shoes other than the boots.

"Where are you going?"

"I thought we covered that." He followed me down the hall. I shrugged him off and checked the charge on my cell. It was on red, but hopefully it had one call left in it. I dialed for a cab.

"Then promise me you'll go to Gabe's," Jamie protested as we stepped outside.

"He's not even home." I gestured to the sun overhead. "Who knows where he sleeps. I'm safer at home, behind my wards."

"What is it about me that offends you so much?"

I turned to stare at him. Hadn't he just said he didn't like me that way? Yet he had that total stalker vibe. No one knew as much about me as he seemed to except maybe Gabe and that often unnerved me too. "Nobody wants to wake up in dirty sheets, Jamie. Do what you will with that."

The cab was quick. I left Jamie open-mouthed, with anger flashing in his eyes. I rode to Gabe's place to retrieve my car, then went home.

The crime scene of my apartment hallway had been cleared. Expedient of them. I was grateful, since I wanted to sink into my own clean bed and read something mindless. After another shower and changing the sheets on my bed, I finally fell into it with a bodice-ripping romance in hand. Later, I'd run again. Maybe find someone who'd fuck me. Someone clean. Which usually meant Gabe. How long would he mourn someone no one really liked? Hopefully it wouldn't take too much to convince him that sex was a better idea, anyway.

Someone knocked on the door. I ignored it, hoping they'd go away. With my luck, it was Jamie again. But the second knock was more insistent. I put the book aside and went to see who was there.

"Seiran Rou, I know you're home," a voice called out. *Shit.*

I threw the door open and shared a glare with my mother, the infamous Tanaka Rou. Her hair was cut in that bobbed-short do that all the celeb girls were sporting. Her stern expression indicated I was in trouble. She looked like a businesswoman, but with the way she ruled the Dominion of the area, you'd have thought she was part dictator.

"I didn't do anything." The denial was out before I even knew what she was going to yell at me for.

She pushed her way inside. Thankfully, I'd set my wards to

welcome her, else there'd have really been a party—probably with her dancing on my intestines. My wards were as strong as I could legally make them, but after endless attacks when I lived on campus, I did everything I was allowed to keep people out of my home. The cops wouldn't do anything, so I learned how to take care of it myself.

"Seiran, it's time you gave up this lifestyle."

"What lifestyle?" I looked at my apartment: clean, semi-stylish furniture, small, but comfortable. Bookcases lined the walls, filled with romance novels and mysteries. "My peculiar choices in reading?"

She stepped toward me, scowling, and I fought the urge not to cower. I had two inches on her, but the habits built over a life-time were hard to break. "I am having a party and I want you to meet some eligible young women. You need a wife to take care of you. You should cut your hair. I don't know why you insist on looking like a girl."

"I was born looking this way. And in case you've forgotten, I'm gay. I like boys. I don't need a wife or a husband. I do just fine on my own." I pulled away from her and headed to the kitchen. "Do you want some coffee?" Manners, damn, manners. How many times had she sat me at a table filled with food, only to slap my hands every time I reached for the wrong fork?

She ignored my question. "What about that vampire boyfriend of yours? Are you still seeing him?"

"I don't have a boyfriend, Mom." With the counter between us, I felt less intimidated, but only a little.

She sat down on one of the barstools looking somewhat like I'd seen other mothers look: worried. I shook my head. The worry made no sense. I remembered her taking a pair of scissors to my hair when I was ten. It hadn't even been that long, but she cut and tore out handfuls, exclaiming that no son of hers would look like a girl. I'd been growing it long since I moved out and still had nightmares that one day she'd return to do the same thing.

"What brings you here?" *How can I make you leave?*

"You should really marry a nice witch. Have babies."

"In that order?"

"Seiran."

"Mom, stop. I don't know what you want. Just tell me, and go away."

"That's rude. I did not raise you to be rude to your elders. I've already told you what I want."

"I'll think about cutting my hair. But I'm not getting married. I don't want babies. I can't imagine how I would screw up a kid. Okay? I'm sorry I can't be the child you wanted."

"It's dangerous for you to be around that vampire." Was she worried about the serial killer from the paper too?

"I'm not. I just work for him. That's all."

"Are you in love with him?"

"Mom, please. I really don't want to talk about my sex life with you."

"So you *are* having sex with him. Are you careful?" Was that actual concern in her voice?

"I'm always careful, Mom."

"How are your studies?" Her change of subjects made my head spin.

"Fine. Same as always." It was irritating that I had to work harder because I was a guy. I had to prove myself to be a Rou just because that's what she demanded I do. As her only child, all the pressure fell to me. "I'm passing everything."

"Good. People expect great things from the Rou line."

"I know."

"Your professor, Dr. Cokota, said you have real promise."

"I just work hard. Get my assignments done. Try to stay out of trouble."

"She treats you fairly? Grades you correctly? She's a strong earth witch."

"Yes, Mom." Though I disagreed about the strong earth witch stuff. Dr. Cokota probably couldn't sense the earth if she had it in a pot growing something beside her.

"You haven't had any trouble here?" She looked over my apartment again with a bit of disgust. I knew it was clean. She'd never find dust in the corners or grime in the sink. No outward flaws—my mother had ingrained that into me at a young age.

"No." No one dared to break in once I moved off campus. I didn't exactly publish to the papers where I lived, either. It was safer that way.

She sighed heavily. "Two earth witches are more likely to produce a powerful child. You should find an earth witch to give you a baby." She got up and moved around the counter, wrapping her arms around me like she was going to hug me. But it was awkward for both of us. She never had been the hugging type, and I had the habit of flinching when she got too close. "Watch your back."

I just nodded and let her out. What had she been warning me for? Was she planning something? It was so strange for her to act like a mother. The weight of the weekend crashed down on me. Someone had killed Frank and left him on my doorstep so I'd be blamed by the police. My mom visited and made it sound like she knew something was going to happen to me, and Gabe was pissed at me 'cause some weird vampire was in town.

Most of my high from the new moon was gone, even though I had one more night to enjoy it. I stared at the abandoned book and the empty bed. The clock ticked just after one in the afternoon. I plugged my phone in to charge and used it to dial a familiar number. He probably wouldn't answer. But it would make me feel better to leave a message.

The phone rang six, seven times, and was halfway through the eighth when a voice said, "Gabe here."

He sounded somewhat disoriented, but I stood there, hoping he would keep talking. "Seiran, is that you?" He seemed to disappear from the phone again, maybe checking the ID. "What's wrong?"

"Nothing," I whispered. But the tremble had already begun. Always after I saw my mom, I was like this. Had my childhood been so bad? I couldn't remember most of it. Just patches. The few bits I had were nightmarish. Like the one about my hair. And there was this other one about a puppy....

"Sei?"

"It's daytime, you can't help."

"Come to my building."

"You can't help, and I don't want to be alone."

"Take the elevator down to the basement. There's a button lock that says B2. Your key will work on it."

"Gabe, I—"

"*Sei.*"

I nodded and hung up the phone, leaving it to charge on the counter, locked up the apartment, then headed to my car, trying not to think much about the past hour. Why seeing my mom and having her touch me was worse than seeing Frank smashed like an unwanted porcelain doll, I didn't know. Maybe Gabe did.

I made record time to his building. Took the elevator down and used the key to his loft upstairs to open the door to the basement, below the underground garage.

This was a different world. Not the showplace from upstairs. Industrial looking. Open, though there were no windows. The kitchen on one end looked high end but unused—glistening stainless steel appliances and sparkling granite counters. Beethoven played from the speakers built into the walls, sounding like a soft lullaby. His furniture, all very different from upstairs, had clean lines but was pale beige. Pops of color came from pillows and a couple of throw blankets that decorated the long sofa and super-wide chaise.

The walls were gray and the floor cedar. The whole place came across as cold, new, but trying to find life. It was so odd.

Gabe leaned against the far wall beside a doorway. His bedroom? Was this Gabe's true home? He looked so natural here. Soft tan pants, a white T-shirt, hair tousled as if from sleep.

"You're trembling." He stood beside me now. Always moved so fast, except when I really needed him to. "Did your mother visit, or was it something else?" His eyes were the pretty green they became when he'd had enough blood. I don't know what I would have said—God only knows how I'd gotten there in one piece—but he kissed me, his lips and tongue taking me over the edge of the madness I clung to. He tasted of copper pennies and Gabe. And I just wanted to be grounded by something.

"Please," I begged when he pulled away.

He kissed me again, sliding his right hand up under my shirt to play with the nipple rings he'd bought me. I grabbed the stupid T-shirt and pulled it over my head, dropping it on his clean living room floor, and reached for his.

"Please." I needed to touch and be touched. Couldn't he see that?

He pulled his shirt off and leaned down for another kiss. That's why I wore the damn boots—I was just too short. I made a frustrated noise, wrapped my hands in his hair, and tried to pull him closer.

"Bedroom," he said.

"I thought you said you sleep with your face to a concrete block," I mumbled, following him to the doorway from which he'd come. The room was small, very gray, with a king-size bed in the middle. Sheets white, pristine. I kicked off my shoes and stripped out of the pants, then pulled at his.

"You're going to be mad at me later for this."

"For what?" I kissed him briefly and shoved the pants off his hips, freeing his large, uncut cock. "So pretty." I didn't give him a chance to answer before taking him into my mouth. He made me stretch in lots of ways. Long and thick, but I'd had a lot of practice swallowing him whole. I could bury my face in his balls and the soft golden pubes, breathing the scent of him while sucking and swallowing around his musky thickness. The thick vein down the center of his cock tasted so salty sweet, and he made lots of fun noises when I paid extra attention to it. My tongue and teeth teased at the foreskin and flicked his dripping slit, his precome a happy flavor in my mouth.

"Christ, Sei," he mumbled, fighting to keep himself upright. "If you don't stop, I won't be fucking you."

"Please," I whispered again, breathing the word across his spit-slicked cock, making him shiver. He pulled away long enough to dig a bottle of lube out of the drawer beside the bed and growled in frustration when the new bottle's plastic seal wouldn't break. Finally it gave, and he poured a bit into his hand before pushing me back and sinking one of his fingers into my ass. The burn and pleasure fought each other, pain losing ground when he hit that spot inside for a brief second before adding a second finger to bring the burn back.

He wasted no time, only giving himself one quick rub with his lubed hand before sliding his cock past the ring of muscle and inside. I pushed back until he was fully sheathed and stroked myself while waiting for him to start pounding me. He stayed still for so long, just staring at me as I looked up at him.

"You're so fucked up, Sei. Beautifully fucked up." And then he took all that amazing lean muscle of his and eased himself into a pounding that had me clinging to him, knees hooked around his elbows, hands in his hair. His stomach muscles caressed my length as he moved in and out, slamming to the core and back again until I came, pouring every bit of myself into that release. Wet heat pooled on my stomach, and he leaned down to kiss me again as his final few strokes took him over the edge and his warmth filled me.

I'd never been a good after-sex talker, and it was almost three in the afternoon, so he must have been tired too. He pulled out and slid behind me, caressing my back and butt crack with his softening cock. And if I hadn't just come, I'd be raring to go again. He just spooned himself around me, arm at my waist, and shrugged the blankets up to cover us both. If this was how the day fucks were, I was so going to need more of these.

CHAPTER 4

My dreams were a bit chaotic, filled with memories from when I was a kid combined with issues I had now. I was usually running from something or someone. In this one, I seemed to know who the serial killer was, but he kept coming after me, so I would run again. I jerked awake at the image of a masked man holding a large knife.

The bedroom was nearly dark. A light glowed from somewhere in the living room area. Gabe was still wrapped around me like a warm cocoon. Odd, since vampires didn't retain heat for long unless they kept drinking blood. I felt a little crusty from the pre-nap sex, but it was an okay feeling since we smelled of sex and us. Underneath, the scent of earth tickled my senses. I reached out with my magic and felt it flow strongly beneath the mattress. The floor was concrete with wood over the top, but somehow I knew there was dirt below the bed. It had the flavor of Gabe's life force—his being—or whatever scientists and magic theorists were calling vampire souls these days.

"Grave dirt?" I asked, not really expecting an answer, though Gabe wasn't asleep. His breathing wasn't deep enough, and even vampires breathed normally when they slept.

"Yes. I tried it upstairs, but the windows don't work for me. The whole bursting into flames thing is a real turn-off." Gabe's voice in my ear was quiet, careful.

"Have you had this place all along?" I glanced back at him. His eyes looked dark in the half-light of the room.

"No. Just finished the renovations last week. I'm thinking about putting the loft up for sale. Unless you want it."

"I have no need for a castle in the sky." My own apartment was a basement room in a house on the edge of a forest. Having the earth close was more than a necessary evil for me. I needed it to breathe most days. "But I thought you liked the loft?"

He said nothing.

I rolled over in his arms, readjusting myself against him. My cock already ached with the need to have him touch me again. He felt interested against me, but nowhere near as interested as I was. I kissed him anyway. "Wanna fuck again?"

Pulling away, he shook his head and got up. "You shower first. You should run again tonight."

"Will you shower with me?" The party seemed to be over. I guess I only got pounded into satisfied oblivion if my mom visited. Maybe I'd have to see her more often. The thought made me shudder.

"I'll take one after you're finished." He sounded detached and careful. Was I missing something?

I headed into the bathroom, which was just as nice as the one he had upstairs, and washed away the sleepiness. The spray of multiple shower-heads flowed nicely in a warm rush on my skin. The water smelled faintly of salt, which meant he probably had a filter and a softener. I basked a little longer than I probably should have. My thoughts focused on this new side of Gabe. It was a bit like he was nesting, perhaps making a permanent place for himself that wasn't a showroom. The whole place just seemed so different, more like my home than Gabe's. Its connection to the earth was calming. We'd been lovers since I'd turned seventeen, and I never imagined he had something like this hiding from me.

Had he done this thinking it would make me commit to him?

When I stepped out of the shower, a clean, white robe in my size had been left on the counter. I dried off and slipped into it, feeling the baby-soft cotton caress my overly sensitive skin. The light in the bedroom had been turned on. The bed was made. Sheets in pale green, the color of new grass, brought some color to the gray walls. A large picture of two men kissing, filled with color and looking very manga-esque, hung over the bed. The closet door stood open to an array of outfits in my size and style. Jeans, dress pants, T-shirts, even a few sweaters and a huge, squared-off section of shoes. No tags, but at least they weren't designer labels. A sick feeling started in my stomach. Gabe leaned against the doorway.

"What is this?"

He shook his head and disappeared out of the room and into the kitchen, where he unpacked bags of groceries. When had he had time to shop?

"Talk to me, Gabe. You're scaring me." I followed him after stepping into a cushy pair of slippers beside the door. "Please tell me you didn't do all this for me."

"I didn't," he said quietly.

He popped open a bottle of QuickLife and tipped it back. I stared at him while he drank and suddenly felt so oddly out of place that I returned to the bedroom and quickly dressed. On the other side of the closet, his things hung in an organized array that mirrored mine. This looked like something very serious. I hurried into an old pair of sneakers and found a light jacket to ward off the night's chill before heading for the door.

"Don't freak out, please," Gabe said from the kitchen behind me.

"I'm not freaking out. I'm just going home."

"We have a date. It's almost seven. The sun will be down in

another forty minutes. We can go to a movie or dancing or something. Unless you just came here for the sex." The last bit sounded bitter.

Shit. I was so not good at this stuff. "Gabe—"

"I'm not asking for anything but what you already promised."

I turned back toward him, feeling trapped and more than a little overwhelmed. The thought of commitment usually did that to me. The apartment was just so much like what I would have chosen and not enough about him that it almost mirrored Jamie's stalking. Was he trying to force himself into my life more than he was? Did he think making an apartment that fit my needs would make me move in? Hadn't we argued that point enough?

"You should see yourself." Gabe moved from behind the counter. "You're terrified. You think I did this all for you. But the bed has a box underneath it, made special. You smelled it."

"Grave dirt."

"Yes. It makes me stronger, and I have to feed less. Being underground means I don't have to hide all day. I can move around freely." He smiled. "The library is yours."

I felt my eyes widen. "Library?"

He nodded toward the closed door on my left. I opened it, and sure enough, it was a room with mostly empty shelves. Only one tall case was full of mystery novels. I recognized a few that I'd bought for him. That growing apprehension was eating at me.

"I gotta go."

"Sure. I'll pick you up at nine. We'll go see that new 3-D kid's movie."

I was already to the door by the time I looked back. He didn't look at me. Just continued to put things away. Cans and boxes. Bananas and a bag of rice. All things I ate. I tried not to think on it too deeply. No words would form while I let myself out and headed to my car. It wasn't like he was tying me up and throwing away the key. He was just making things more comfortable. For both of us. Maybe.

CHAPTER 5

F inding Detective Andrew Roman outside my apartment
didn't calm my nerves at all. Was he back to arrest me?

"Your mother has asked the police to back off. Convenient
having a family member with so much power."

I unlocked my door. "So why are you here? There's no way
that I could've killed Frank. And why would I? Now I'll have to
do his shifts at work too."

"Can I come in?"

"No." My wards and the threshold would keep him out, but I
didn't really want the police pounding down the door, either.
"What do you want?"

"I want to talk about your power."

"I'm an earth witch. It runs in the family. Talk to my mom."

"What about your dad? Where's he?"

"Again, talk to my mom. I have no clue who my sperm donor
was. I suspect she probably killed him when she had me instead
of some bouncing baby girl." I stepped inside and flicked the light
on. Thankfully everything looked in its place, and the magic of
my wards tingled familiar and safe around me.

"I'd really like to talk further about your magic. Perhaps you'll tell me how often you have the need to shift? All three days of the new moon?"

Breathing was hard for a few seconds while I struggled to try to remain calm. He'd know. He was a vampire. He could hear my pulse speed up. "I don't know what you're talking about."

"The Dominion has been looking for an earth Pillar for years. Your mom isn't strong enough to act as focus for all the other earth witches in our region. The current earth Pillar, Rose, is nowhere near as powerful as you."

"That has nothing to do with me."

"You're powerful enough to be the earth Pillar."

Did he want me dead? "No man shall act as focus or lead a Dominion coven in any elemental magic. It's the fifth sacred law."

"The first sacred law being thou shall not slip thy skin to run as a beast for any time except those who are lycan born of the moon. Funny how all their laws end in death for doing something that is natural to a witch. Any witch higher than level three will change into something."

At least he was just speculating about my change. I'd have sensed him if he'd followed me when I ran with Jamie last night. I shrugged. "It's like chocolate. Just because it tastes good doesn't mean you should eat the whole box."

He smiled and leaned against the outside of my doorway. It seemed so fake—like he was putting on an act for me. Maybe it was because he was so old he didn't know how to be human anymore. Or maybe he was just trying to be a nice guy when all he wanted to do was rip my throat out. I wondered if Gabe had ever looked that put-on for me and I'd just ignored it or didn't notice. All I knew for sure was that Andrew Roman gave me a bad vibe.

"And how often do you taste the chocolate, Seiran?"

"I don't. My mom is one of the council members for the Dominion. I'd be first on the chopping block. Now go away. I have a date to get ready for."

"Santini?"

"I don't see why that's any of your business." I moved to shut the door, but the look of anger that crossed his face made me pause. Fuck but I didn't need another crazy man in my life. "What do you want from me?"

"All in good time. All in good time, Seiran Rou." He turned away and headed down the hallway. I shut the door, double-locked it, and headed for the bathroom to brush out my tangled hair. It'd probably take me until Gabe arrived to make it presentable. But at least the power of earth wasn't riding me so hard tonight.

The next knock on my door made me feel very popular—and annoyed. If Roman had returned, he'd better have a warrant or I'd be calling the cops on him.

I dropped the brush on the bed and went to the door, hoping Gabe was early. It swung open, and oddly enough, Brown Hair from the bar stood there. Brock, wasn't it? He gripped a potted ivy plant. His smile looked awkward on his very young face. He glanced over me from head to toe again and swallowed back a bigger smile.

He held the plant out to me. "Here, it's for you. Because you're an earth witch, I thought you might like things that grow, rather than cut flowers or something."

I must have blinked at him for too long without taking it, because he set the plant down beside the door and backed away. What was it with people stalking me?

"Thanks, Brock."

His smile grew a hundred percent. "You remembered my name."

"Sure. How'd you find where I live?" He was into me. I got that from his stare, but it was more than a little creepy.

He shoved his hands in his pockets. "You were on the news. Well, sort of. They talked about that other waiter from Bloody

Bar being killed, and the reporters showed the building where it happened. You were headed to your car."

I'd been on camera? What the hell? Didn't my mom have people monitoring the news just to keep me off camera? She hated cleaning up whatever media mess I caused without trying, so everything about me was supposed to be screened before it went to air. Apparently something had gotten through. Which meant I'd have to call her—fuck.

"What are you doing here? You don't really seem the type to date guys. And I'm not really the kind of guy that's good with breaking in virgins."

Brock flushed and swept his hands through his hair. "It's not like that. I just wanted to talk to you. I mean, you're a male witch! No one can do that. My mom is a witch, but I have no power. I'd be lucky to light a match."

Fire, eh? "So you're like a groupie? Did you and your friends come into the bar just for that?"

"To see you, yes. There's been a lot of talk around campus. We all watch the girls pile into the magic studies classes. You're the only guy with enough balls to pick up the books and go too. We thought it was just because of your mom. But you're really something special."

"I bet you say that to all the boys."

He frowned. "It's true."

"Thanks for the plant, Brock." I toed the plant in through the door and made to shut it. "It's probably best you don't come around again. People tend to get hurt when they linger in my life."

His outstretched hand stopped the door, and for once I wondered if my wards were strong enough to keep out an intruder like him. They hadn't been made to keep out average humans. Vampires, shifters, and high-level witches, yes, but not a football player. He wasn't a huge guy. Maybe close to six feet tall, a hundred and eighty pounds. He looked like a runner, maybe a quarterback. Sporty and muscular. And part witch. If he had just talked to me at school instead of following me to my workplace and finding out where I lived, I might have invited him in.

"I didn't mean to upset you," he said.

"I'm not upset. I just have to get ready. A friend is coming to see me."

"A lover?"

"Not really your business, Brock." I felt the sun set and the power begin to rise again. Inside the building, I really couldn't do much to him without destroying my home. Outside, I could have pulled roots from the ground or had a large tree swat him away. That stupid ivy plant did me no good. A trained witch would know that. But I was the only trained male witch around, right?

"Maybe we could have coffee sometime." He took a step forward.

I put myself behind the door and pulled energy up through the ground to make my body like a rock behind it. "I don't think that's a good idea. You and I aren't in the same circles."

He looked disappointed but didn't try to force his way in. "You mean because you're first wave?"

I was a first-generation earth witch—first wave. It was a bit like an old-fashioned aristocracy. Anyone not first wave was thought of as less by most. None of that mattered to me. A male witch was bottom of the barrel anyway. "No. I mean 'cause you're a jock and I'm just a pretty boy-whore. We're an odd couple that's just not meant to mix."

"I heard you used to run," Brock pointed out.

Before my mother's white room and after my years with Matthew, running had been an outlet. Now it was just exercise. "Not really. Have a good night." I made to shut the door again.

"Maybe another time."

"Do you want the plant back?" I asked him.

"No. It's for you." He turned away and headed down the hall, looking uncertain and seeming to want to come back again, but I closed the door and locked it. For once I regretted all the flirting I did at the bar. I picked up my brush and tackled the rest of the tangles in my hair.

The clock ticked past nine fifteen, and I began to worry. Gabe was never late. I checked the mirror again. I looked all right, had decided to tone down the wardrobe for the evening: faded blue jeans and a white cashmere sweater with light brown, short, hiking shoes. Gabe had said we were going to a kid's movie. When the knock finally came, I let out the breath I didn't know I'd been holding.

I opened the door, expecting Gabe, but Jamie stood there. "What the hell? Where's Gabe?"

"He's fine. Just had to do some vamp stuff. So he asked me to take you to the movie and drop you off at his place later." He wore brown leather pants like a second skin over that huge bulge he always had and a fishnet-looking brown sweater. Date clothes, probably.

"Thought you didn't like me that way?"

"It's just a movie, Seiran. I'd like to get to know you better. Gabe had something come up. And I've spent most of the day training the temps Gabe hired for the bar, just so he could have the night off to spend with you."

"Yet he's not here." I was more upset than I thought I should be. After all, I was the one who kept saying we weren't dating. And here I was, becoming the clingy type I so hated. I'd just spent the last hour agonizing over what to wear because I'd wanted to look good for him, and now he wasn't coming.

"You look nice tonight. You should dress like this more often."

I ignored him, locked up the apartment, and waved at him to get moving.

He paused and put his hands out to each side like he was

searching for approval. "Do I smell okay? Look okay? I don't want to embarrass you."

What the hell? I never knew what to make of him. "You're kind of creepy."

"I'm okay with that." He headed down the hall, motioning me to follow.

Neither of us spoke until we were in the car. "Let's go to the bar," I told him.

"Why?"

Because having new people manning the bar when I was not there made me nervous. What if they didn't wash the dishes or something? "I just need to check on it, okay? Humor me."

Jamie shrugged and pointed the car in the direction of the bar. When we arrived, the lot was full. Typical Sunday night. I stepped inside, breathing that familiar scent of smoke and unwashed people. Two waitresses I didn't recognize worked the room, but the bartender was Michael Fawn, a vampire Gabe had "brought over." He didn't work much but always came when Gabe asked. He just nodded his dark head at me and went back to filling drinks.

I journeyed the whole way around, even checking the kitchen to be sure Rick and José were still manning the stove and fryer. Rick waved a spatula at me and gave me some crap about it being my night off. The kitchen was as clean as always. Spotless, as Gabe demanded. The dishes swished in the washer, and everything was in its place. It was the cleanest professional kitchen I'd ever seen. And since I was a neat freak, that meant something.

Jamie leaned against the wall outside the kitchen smiling at me. "Everything okay?"

"Yeah. Yeah." The crowd was mostly regulars tonight. But a few unusuals had wandered in. Brock's crowd was back, though he seemed to be working very hard to ignore me. And my Earth Magic Studies teacher, Professor Cokota, sat at the bar, munching on fries and drinking a glass of white wine. She smiled in my direction.

I stepped up beside her. "Please tell me you're not here because of my mom, Professor."

"Julia," she said. "Please call me, Julia. You're not working tonight?"

"No. I have a date tonight." She couldn't have been a very powerful earth witch, or else she wouldn't be here drinking away her troubles. She'd be outside communing with the earth.

"With that pretty blond man over there?" Her eyes looked over Jamie like he was some sort of cut of meat hung for auction. Did I look at people that way? A woman who liked men like Jamie didn't much like men like me.

"He's just the chauffeur."

She put her hand over mine, and a tiny twinge of earth rolled between us. It was small, not nearly the power that Jamie and I had playfully rolled back and forth last night. Obviously she wasn't as powerful as she claimed to be. "I could be your date tonight."

I pulled away from her. "My mom put you up to this."

"She did suggest that you and I might make a good couple. You're a Rou, Seiran. You should be married already. Producing an heir. Not sitting in some classroom with a bunch of nobodies." She said my name wrong again.

"It's Say-ron. Not See-rin. There will be no Rou heirs from me. If I have my way, the line will die with me. Doesn't the university have a no-fraternizing-with-students rule? Or do you think by marrying me, you'll never have to work again? I guess the joke's on you then since I don't work here for my health. My mother gives me nothing. I'll see you in class tomorrow, Professor Cokota. Have a nice evening."

She glared at me as I walked away. Must have hit the nail on the head with that one. A lot of girls looked my way until they found out that being with me didn't get them the Rou fortune.

My mother believed hard work was the only way anyone should get money—including me.

I grabbed Jamie and headed toward the door feeling like a hundred eyes were on me. The new moon power was stilted tonight—like it was far away—until I stepped outside and it hit me like an iron safe to the head. I paused in the middle of the parking lot to bask in the power. It had to have been blocked while I was inside.

"We should go," Jamie whispered to me. "I can take you for a run if you want."

"Who warded the bar?" I wondered out loud.

"Me."

"Against earth magic?"

"All magic. Mostly violence. Though it still gets through. You probably could have done better and created stronger wards, but I made do. It makes it easier for you to work, since we're on the edge of the city. The earth doesn't press on you so hard inside, right?" Jamie tromped to his car and got in the driver's side. "Let's go."

I nodded, got in, and buckled up, feeling the night pull at me. Running didn't appeal. Something else did, but not with Jamie. He set my creep-meter off a hundred percent. "Do you do that sort of thing for Gabe?"

"No. Everything I do is for you."

Okay. Two hundred percent. "You're so creepy. I probably shouldn't be in the car with you."

"Yet you are. Why?"

"Gabe trusts you."

"And for all the smack you talk, you trust Gabe."

"Yes. Maybe he doesn't know how you're stalking me."

Jamie smiled and started the car. "He knows. The only person you're safer with than me is Gabe."

"You don't make me feel all that safe. Can you take me to Gabe?"

"He's doing vampire business."

"What if I want to keep him safe?"

"He's a vampire. They're really hard to kill."

"Yeah, only fire or total body destruction. I took Metaphysics 101. But just because he's strong doesn't mean someone can't hurt him. You told me not to trust that Andrew Roman guy. He seems to not like Gabe. Is that who his business is with?"

"You talk like you care. Aren't you the guy who's so anti-relationship you don't sleep with the same guy twice? Except Gabe, of course. But even him you keep at arm's length. Why?"

The reasons were too many and too graphic to articulate. I stared out the window instead. "Just take me to him, please. I did promise him we'd go out tonight."

Jamie shrugged, and soon enough, we were parked downtown and walking toward a club that reverberated with power —Loco Mojo. It was a grunge club for vamps and lycans. I'd been there before with a lycan date or two. Had a spell that could make me pass for that otherworldly feeling they had. Tonight I didn't even need it since the earth circled through me in a loop that would have made most shifters howl at the moon —if there had been one. The guard nodded to Jamie and let us in.

Music wailed through the club in that angry-guitar-and-thumping-drum-beat way. Bodies gyrated like tribal people of cultures millennia past. Lust strangled the scents of leather and sweat.

Gabe stood near a booth toward the back, but thankfully, none of the other vampires with him looked like Andrew Roman. Gabe wore black leather pants and just a spiked collar. His pretty eyes were darkened to the vampire black I knew to mean hunger. But he gripped a QuickLife, type AB. Not his favorite.

I was moving in his direction before I even realized it, and he met me halfway. He quirked an eyebrow at me and set the bottle on the tray of a busboy walking by.

"This club is vamp and lycan only. No humans allowed, witch or not." He glared at Jamie behind me, who just shrugged.

I pressed my body against his and felt him grow hard beneath that leather. My blood pounded. Touching him was like sinking my toes into freshly dug earth. I needed him like I needed to breathe.

I was wearing too much today, dammit. I tore the sweater off, pressed my chest to his, and kissed him. "Won't you make an exception for me?" The innocent words pressed from my lips to his. The garbled reply that fell from him was too primal to be a protest.

He dragged me away from the tables and dance floor toward one of the back rooms that were known for privacy. I unzipped his pants and let him spring free of the confines to press into my hand. His growl warned me just before he slammed the door open, pressed me into the opposite wall, and kicked the door shut. The five-by-six room with a short bench and a cushy rug wasn't much on romance, but neither of us needed psychological foreplay tonight.

"You really shouldn't have come here," he whispered to me. "It's not safe."

I kissed him and played with him—stroking his length in a strong twist from base to tip. He pushed me onto the seat and undid my jeans.

I said, "You keep saying that, but I haven't met anyone who seems to be out to hurt me." A couple of weird stalker types who seemed interested in sex maybe, but not out to hurt me.

"Serial killer, remember?" He stroked me hard enough to make it difficult to remember my name.

I shrugged and licked one of his nipples, rolling my tongue around it. Again he lost speech to those lustful sounds. The other nipple received the same treatment. "You talk too much," I told him.

"Mhmm" was all he mumbled before bowing his head and

taking my hard cock into his mouth, swallowing down to the root. I released his cock and dug my hands into his hair, fighting the urge to thrust into that handsome face. Being a vampire gave him sharper canines than most, so oral could be dangerous. But his mouth knew skill I could only dream of, and I was coming so fast it made me dizzy.

He swallowed it all down and licked me clean before tucking me away and zipping up my jeans. I felt like a limp noodle, so I let him, and just smiled. In a minute or two I would be able to return the favor. He kissed me lightly, lips trailing over my collarbone. The sharp pressure of his teeth was the only warning of his bite before flesh gave way, and the draw of his mouth made me tremble. I closed my eyes to the sensation of him drawing my blood into himself. It was always sort of erotic. Though Gabe was the only one I'd ever experienced that with. I'd had other vampires, but never let them drink from me. It was too intimate and it gave them power over me.

"And you call me evil," I told him when he finished. He licked away the tiny trails of blood from the already-healing bite and kissed me again, eyes green now.

"You will probably be the death of me." He shook himself out. His cock throbbed hard and red now, filled with my blood. The thought began to awaken my body from the satisfied lethargy. I was up for another round if he was.

"That was crazy."

"I told you; no humans allowed," Gabe said.

I blinked at him. "I've been here before."

"Not on the new moon. You know lycans put your power into high gear on a normal day. During the new moon—"

I laughed and ran my hands along the strong lines of his bare chest. The scar below his left breast had always fascinated me. He'd been a soldier or something back in classical Rome. But he never talked about it. "The last day of the new moon is tonight.

You, near naked, within my reach, is more than enough to kick me off the edge. Let's make the earth move."

He frowned. "I don't think you know what you're saying."

I dropped to my knees and took him into my mouth.

Gabe tried to pull away but ended up bracing himself against the wall just to keep standing in sort of a half push-up. "At least you could have siphoned off some of this energy before you came. Or were you worried about me?"

I brushed my tongue over his tip, teasing his foreskin, and he jerked. I held tight, fisting a large portion of him in my grasp. He dripped with my spit as I pulled off to say, "Worked off the energy with whom? Jamie? I suppose he'd do in a pinch."

A look of jealous rage crossed his face. "You didn't...."

I smiled and swallowed around him. Someone knocked on the door, and a second later it opened a bit. Jamie peered at us, his long hair falling around him. "Everything okay?" he asked, his eyes only briefly dropping to me.

Gabe reached back and slammed the door shut. "Sei can't talk. His mouth is full."

Jamie's laughter echoed through the door. He obviously wasn't going away. I closed my eyes and set myself to the task at hand. Or in this case, in hand. But Gabe pulled away and stuffed himself back inside his pants. Surprisingly, the leather covered him up, and I could hardly tell he was rock hard under all that black.

"But—" I tried to protest. He really wasn't going to let me finish him?

He yanked me to my feet, opened the door a crack, and said, "His sweater?"

Jamie shoved my white sweater through the door, then it shut again.

Gabe tugged it over my head, and I shrugged into it. "You don't want me to suck you off? I'll be fast, I promise," I said, probably sounding like a child denied candy.

"Another time. Go to a movie with Jamie, please. I will see you later. Let me finish my work here."

He opened the door, and Jamie stood there, trying to look neutral. Not that he wasn't attractive, but I just didn't want to go anywhere with him. Gabe pushed me forward. "Take him to a movie or something. I'll call when I'm done with business and pick him up."

"What am I? Some kind of latchkey kid?" But both of them ignored me.

Jamie gripped my arm and dragged me toward the door. Gabe disappeared farther into the club. What the hell was going on with everyone lately?

Back in the car with Jamie was one of the last places I wanted to be. "Take me home," I told him.

"Gabe said—"

"Take me home, or I'm calling a cab." I wanted to cry for some reason. Was it the rejection? Gabe told me no pretty regularly. Often put me off only to deliver on the promise later. But he'd been acting odd all weekend. I wondered again if he was trying to find a way to end our not-relationship. But that didn't make sense with all the work he just did to make his apartment fit me. And then I realized that wondering if he was ending things sort of made it a relationship, didn't it? Fuck.

Jamie sighed and started the car, then headed for my apartment in the boonies. Flashing lights brightened the area for miles around my place. As we turned into the parking lot, I realized they had swarmed my building, and my heart sped up.

Cops directed our car to the back of the lot. Guns drawn, they told us to get out and put our hands up. Maybe it would have been a better idea to go to a movie….

We got out, were searched for weapons and forced to kneel on the ground with our hands on our heads like criminals. I'd never felt quite so afraid before. Sure, I expected the Dominion to someday come for me, but not with flashing lights and weapon-wielding cops.

Andrew Roman appeared among the group. "Come with me." His hand was more than a little rough as he yanked me to my feet.

Jamie began to protest, but the cops surrounding him threatened violence if he didn't stay down.

I followed Roman up through the line of police, medics, and shocked apartment dwellers, down the hall to my place, feeling more than a little lightheaded myself.

The scene at the door nearly brought me to my knees.

Apparently, my wards had worked.

The door to my apartment lay on its side in the hallway. Brownish-red fluid ran free from the doorway, like a bubbling mass trying to escape. It stained the carpet into the hall for several feet. It was like a gruesome episode of a crime show where someone had just exploded spontaneously and left a mess behind.

A cop flew by me, face green and appearing to be fighting the urge to vomit. All I could smell was shit and blood. My heart beat like it was trying to escape my chest.

I approached the door with a suffocating sense of dread, wondering how bad it would be. The wards weren't supposed to be lethal. They were just set to stun anyone who entered without my permission. And keep stunning them until they left, or I made them leave. Anything not human couldn't enter at all. It would be like trying to go through a brick wall. I'd set it that way for witches too, level three or higher.

Roman gestured toward the doorway. I glanced inside, but what was there, the red mess that my apartment had become, didn't make sense. "Undo the wards so we can get the medics in there," Roman told me.

I blinked at him, not understanding at first. If that was a person in there, then they were dead. I didn't need my nose to tell me that since whatever was left was nothing but a mess of pieces. Medics couldn't help them now. But my wards hadn't been set to do anything like that.

"Seiran, undo the wards." Roman's voice was softer this time, his hand on my shoulder.

I touched my palm to the edge of the doorsill and shut each of the wards off, like turning off a light. When they were all down, I nodded to Roman, who put his hand out and felt the open doorway, then gestured to the cops who had followed us into the hall. Several medics and cops went into the apartment. Two more came toward me, cuffs out.

"I didn't do this," I heard myself say, a shake begin in my hands, and I hadn't even seen my mother yet. "My wards weren't strong enough to hurt anyone." By themselves they were legal magic. But the many different flavors I'd laid, one across another, probably weren't. I let the cops cuff me, heard them read me my rights, and knew that when they put me in the car, there would be a witch with me. Probably an air or fire witch to keep me from hurting others, since they considered me rogue now.

A rogue male witch.

The world hadn't had one of those in probably four or five decades. I should have felt something, but with my heart pounding so hard, the only emotion I could find was fear.

Jamie looked horrified when the cops led me out to the squad car. There were camera flashes and questions shouted from the line of reporters that had appeared.

Witch executions were always conducted the traditional way —burning at the stake. I wondered how quickly my mom would work to get my execution moved up. The whole world seemed to lose focus and move, like a soundless movie picture.

CHAPTER 6

The police station was a lot more of the same. They put me in a warded cell and closed the door, which hit me like a slap in the face, because it cut me off from the Earth and from life in general. I stared at the mirror across the room, knowing there were probably eyes glaring at me through it, but no one entered the room.

When the door finally opened, I felt like I'd been sitting there for hours. Andrew Roman stood there alone, notebook in one hand, cup in the other. He set the cup down in front of me. It was coffee, black. I couldn't drink coffee black. I couldn't imagine drinking anything right now. The sick feeling in my stomach just made me want to puke from looking at that cup. The mess of my apartment didn't make sense, and I kept trying not to think about it because I didn't want it to come together in my head.

"I want you to be honest with me, Seiran. Your friend Jamie Browan says the two of you were together tonight and that you were at Loco Mojo for a while. That can be confirmed, but doesn't clear you of setting illegal wards."

"My wards were all legal. Set to stun. Nonentry to vampires and lycans."

"And witches."

"Witches level three and above. Witches don't like me much. I stayed in the dorms my first year of college. People kept stealing things, vandalizing my room, and put hexes on me. Witches. They didn't like that I was a guy and among them."

"Is that why you killed Professor Cokota?"

Cokota? That thing in my house had been the professor? Images of the red mess started to pull together in my head. Thankfully, a small metal trash can sat in the corner of the room. I spewed the little I'd eaten that day and dry heaved for several minutes before feeling my stomach start to relax. But I knew it was just the first wave of what was sure to be many.

Roman politely held my hair back. He even took the can away and returned with a fresh one and a wet cloth. "Sit, please. I'd like to ask a few questions."

The cloth did nothing to clean the acid taste out of my mouth. I sat back down at the table. My hands shook so hard I put them in my lap. "I didn't kill anyone. My wards weren't—"

"She was shoved through your wards, Seiran. Like a block of cheese through a grater."

My stomach convulsed again. I fought it, kept the cloth to my mouth, fist clenched against my thigh, and tried to push the revulsion down.

"If you can prove the wards were no more than level two, then we may be able to make a case of accidental death. You'd get a few years of jail time, probably out on good behavior in six months. You know the Dominion doesn't mess around with magic. Level-two wards for protection are standard. Anything higher is overkill. But death by magic, even accidental, is punishable by the Dominion."

I just shook my head, not knowing what to say. I'd burn for this. Even if someone else had killed her, they'd used my magic and I'd be the one to burn.

"What about the serial killer?" I whispered. Could I do jail?

Six months or more of not being outside or able to change would probably kill me. And all the metal. What if they put me in a cell not on the first floor? Panic began to curl deep within my gut.

"What do you mean, what about the serial killer? What serial killer would this be?"

"The one who's been killing people around vampires. Professor Cokota was at the Bloody Bar tonight. Maybe he saw her and thought she was a vampire groupie, so he killed her." It sounded like a stretch, even to me.

"And conveniently knew your apartment had wards stronger than level two against witches in which to kill her?" He flipped through something in his notebook. "Your professor had you ranked as a level-three earth witch. That's the highest any male has ranked in more than half a century."

I said nothing. The test results were a lie. I'd purposely scored low, but he didn't need to know that. No one needed to know that. But I didn't like where the questioning was going. Should I ask for a lawyer? Isn't that what people did on TV?

"She also had notes that hypothesized you purposely get answers wrong in tests to keep yourself ranked low. She speculated that you were at least a level-four witch, possibly a level five. Is that correct, Mr. Rou?"

My heart sank and head spun. Had I done something obvious? Or had she been guessing? Oh sweet Gaea, if my mom found out...

The door slammed open, and my mom stood there, a police sergeant behind her and another man in a suit behind him. Roman stood up. "I'm not finished questioning him yet."

My mother moved across the room and around the table. I jumped up from the chair and backed away. She was going to kill me. I just knew it. For years she'd been searching for a reason. Now she had it, and she was going to rip me apart.

I trembled and cowered in the corner. "I didn't do it. I didn't do anything wrong!"

The man in the suit got between the two of us and said something hushed to my mother. She looked angry but backed away. The sergeant was talking to Roman in angry tones. I couldn't make out any of the words.

"Seiran, come with me, please," the man in the suit told me quietly. He reached out a hand to help me up, but I couldn't. My body shook like I was on the verge of some horrible seizure, and all I could think about was how I was going to burn.

My mom just stood there looking so angry. I put my head in my hands, but couldn't stop shaking. In school they made us watch public executions of witches. By the time I was ten, I'd seen more than a half dozen. The screams always got to me first. They echoed in my memory and made me sob like a baby. Gabe had said the smell was worse and lasted for weeks. Thankfully I'd only ever seen the burnings on TV. Except now I'd be at my own —smelling myself burn. Maybe the smoke would kill me quickly. Or maybe Gabe could slip me something that killed me before the fire even started. He'd do that for me, right? He cared about me. No matter how hard I pushed him away, he still cared.

I barely noticed a couple of medics who'd come in the room until they grabbed me and jabbed a needle in my arm. My mom approached again, and I fought to pull away, but was yanked down into unnatural, dreamless darkness.

I woke up feeling groggy. Brightness made me cringe and blink back tears when I finally opened my eyes. The bright white of the room stood as a horrific reminder of my past. I'd been here before.

In high school I'd floated, not really having any friends, but no longer bullied because I fought back when people tried to push me around. My senior year I looked at different courses and colleges. Considered a lot of career paths. Decided on health and nutrition and began searching for the right school. Then I made the mistake of telling my mom.

This room is where I'd ended up. Four white walls, fluorescent lights glaring overhead, me in the middle of the room, strapped to a gurney. I tested the movement of my body and found myself tied down, just like the last time, arms at my sides, restraints in three places, and the same around my legs. The two across my torso made it difficult to get full breaths, and the one around my forehead kept me from turning left or right to look at the room. Not that it mattered: the room was empty. It had a concrete floor and was located on the second story, away from all plant life or anything that might offer me earth power.

My first visit had been a test of wills. Nearly three weeks, Mom kept me here, until I agreed to go to the school for magic despite the fact that I was male. I was a Rou after all.

This time I knew I couldn't take weeks or even days of this. I'd go mad. The earth was so far away, and yet I knew the moon was still absent. Darkness blanketed my part of the world, and most of it slept.

A constant pounding set my head to ache. I knew distantly that the sound was just my heart beating. And that within a few hours I'd tune it out and then go crazy trying to hear it again.

But nothing could be worse than the growing need to urinate. The pressure would eventually be too much, and then the filth and stench would cover me. I'd been here before. Still I fought the need. Oh Gaea, how long could I last? If this was to be my fate, I'd rather burn.

The door opened, and a bit of that earth moved closer, even as the door closed again. I couldn't see him until he stepped up beside me. Gabe's blond curls looked a mess, but he was dressed normally now and looked very tired. Maybe being able to move around during the day wasn't such a good thing for him. Vampires needed rest too. Like humans deprived of sleep, vampires could become weaker.

I couldn't think of a single reason why he'd be here, in my mother's house.

"Sei? You in there?"

I sighed as heavily as my restraints would allow and mumbled, "I'm awake."

He looked relieved. "This is very bad."

"Professor Cokota died." Flashes of images from my flat were there but pushed back somehow. I couldn't get a grasp on them, and for that I was grateful. "I didn't kill her."

"No one thinks you did. Your mother believes someone is trying to frame you." He gripped my hand, settling a good link to the earth around me. If he stayed, I might be able to bear it a little longer. "But the wards you were using were too high a level to be ignored."

"But people used to attack me. I filed police reports. Dozens of them. Doesn't that matter?" I wanted to move, thrash, anything but be stuck in this immobile white world again. "Please help me. We can run away. I'll go wherever you want."

Gabe smiled lightly, though it looked strained. "You're saying you'll run away with me? That sounds like commitment, Sei."

Tears burned at the edge of my eyes. I didn't want him to see me cry or beg, like the whimpering thing I would become if I stayed here. "Please. I'll do whatever you want. Be whatever you want. Just don't leave me here." I'd die. I knew it wouldn't even take days this time. Just a few hours of absolute misery before my heart gave out and I withered away to nothing.

Gabe was quiet for a few minutes. Tears seeped down my cheeks. He didn't want me, did he? I'd pushed him away too much and made him angry. Now my mother had dragged him into all this when he probably just wanted to be free of my stupid issues.

"You say sweet things when coerced."

"I say sweeter things when you fuck me. So let's escape and do that."

"And if what I ask is for you to commit to me?"

For as long as that lasted, whatever, sure. "Yes. Anything."

His smile was a little sad. "You're a horrible liar, Sei."

"I'll stay as long as you want me."

He nodded this time. "And you think that won't last long." He sighed. "If you agree to give your mom an heir, she will ask the council for a pardon based on the prior attacks and your current mental state."

"I'm gay. That's not a mental problem."

"She means your paranoia and OCD, not your homosexuality. She said she will pick a suitable mother—"

"I can't marry anyone. I'm gay. I'd make any woman miserable." *Probably most men, too.*

"Marriage is not required. Just a child. She said she will raise the baby herself if need be, so you don't have to be bothered." Gabe gripped my hand tighter, like he was trying to tell me something.

"Unless it's a boy, and then she would torture him like she did me."

"Sei, I can compel you to do this. I'd rather you just give in and let her have what she wants. Then I can take you out of here, and you can go on living your life like you were."

"I can go back to school, where everyone stares like I'm a freak? Back to the bar to bus tables to pay for an apartment I can never go home to? What do I have left?"

"Your freedom. It's 2:00 a.m., and your body is suffering already from being so far from the earth. You're so pale I could trace every vein with my fingers. That's why your mom let me in. You give her this, and she will ensure you walk free. This isn't like when you were in high school. Your power is too strong. You'd be dead in a day or two if she kept you here. And I'm out of options." Gabe looked up toward the door, but I couldn't turn my head to see what he saw.

A baby. I could sit here forever, rot in my own stench, and

starve if she forced me to go days without food, like before. Give a child to one of the cruelest mothers in the world, or stay here until I died. Getting burned at the stake had to be better than this. "Fine. I will give her an heir."

Gabe smiled for real this time, looking relieved.

Someone else appeared on my other side, and I couldn't keep from flinching. It was my mother. She looked stern as usual. "An heir?" she asked Gabe.

"He agreed."

"Seiran?"

"Yes, fine. Whatever. They can do that artificial-like nowadays, right? Whatever." I clenched my eyes shut, trying not to think about the white box around me. If I ever got furniture again, it wouldn't be white. My lungs hurt from lack of air. I just needed to be free. To run. Even if that was away from all of this.

"And I want you to test again."

I opened my eyes and looked at her. "Test what?"

"Your magic levels. No throwing the tests this time."

My head was already shaking a no in the tiny centimeter of space I had under the restraints before she could finish speaking. No way in hell I was going to let anyone know what I could really do. Gabe gripped my hand tighter.

"You change two, sometimes three nights of the new moon," my mother said.

My heart pounded. Was she having someone follow me? Did she know how hard it was for me to stay human those nights? The way the power pushed me to the very limits of my human brain?

"The sacred vows are in place to keep low-level witches from trying something they won't recover from." Her heels clacked on the hard floor, and the sound bounced around the room. I couldn't see her but knew she wasn't leaving anytime soon. "How often do you have to change? And don't lie to me, Seiran. Your life is already in my hands."

I knew she meant it too. Being the leader of the region's Dominion, she could take over any magic-related case. Her say was law. Sadly, she'd never used that to help me when I was in trouble before. Was she really going to get me out of it this time?

Gabe nodded, encouraging me to answer. I sighed and said, "At least twice. Sometimes all three nights." Three nights if I didn't have enough sex to bleed off the energy the earth poured into me.

"What level were your wards?"

"Two." I knew better. Always by the book. "They were all level two. I just set more of them. *Do what thou wilt, though it harm none.* I followed the rules. The Code has nothing against setting multiple wards."

She stepped up beside me. "You'll test. And I want the heir."

"Sure. I'll take the stupid test and donate my sperm."

"Any male child remains with him," Gabe interrupted.

"And he shall then try for another, until a female is born." My mother and Gabe glared at each other over me.

"Done," Gabe said.

I wanted to protest, since he was pimping me out as some sort of stud, but he just looked at me with those pretty green eyes— silently pleading.

"You can let him go, then," my mother said, probably not willing to chip a nail by touching the restraints. She stared at me like I was a bug in a jar that she was waiting to suffocate.

Gabe immediately started to loosen the straps. I felt the ones around my chest slacken first and sucked in a deep breath. Then the restraint around my head disappeared. I closed my eyes and waited until the straps were all gone before opening them again and rolling off the gurney, into Gabe's arms. My legs shook so hard I couldn't stand. The white walls and floor still seemed to be closing in.

"I'm taking him to my house. You have my number. We'll set up a time for the test—supervised, of course—and we'll leave choosing a suitable surrogate to you." Gabe held me up with an arm firmly around my waist. I fought to stay conscious while so many nightmares replayed.

"He will be in school tomorrow," my mom said.

My head spun. How could I think about school now? The world wanted me dead and now I had to somehow make a baby. Fuck, my head hurt.

"There may not be any school tomorrow since his teacher was murdered."

"But he will be there, ready to attend. He's a Rou, and his only crime is paranoia. I will be sure to speak to the press. My official statement will clear him of any wrongdoing. The police can continue to look at other angles." She glared at us.

Gabe ran his fingers through my hair, body pressed tightly to mine. I wanted to sink into his strong arms and forget the troubles of the world for a while. "I'll have Jamie take him to school and pick him up afterward. You'll agree that he is someone's target? That too much time in public is dangerous right now? Since you want an heir."

"Agreed."

"Great. You know where to find us." He began to shuffle me toward the doorway. I clung to him like he was all I had left.

"Indeed."

By the time we made it outside, I was a quivering mass of jelly. I couldn't even walk. The earth slammed into me with such a force, I dropped to my knees. I needed to shift. Soon, if not now. Gabe pulled me up and dragged me to his car. "Hold back, Sei. We need to get the hell out of Dodge."

And then we were driving. Obviously not toward his loft or new basement home. Nor could we go back to my home. I didn't think I could ever go back there. Maybe I could talk someone into getting my stuff for me.

Gabe hit a button, and the window on my side rolled down. If I'd been a dog, I would have hung my head out just to breathe in the smell of earth. Instead I let the breeze pour over me, drowning me in power as we flew past houses and paved lots until trees began to surround us.

"Are we running?" I finally asked when we hit open road and crossed the border into Wisconsin.

"Yes and no," Gabe answered. "Take out your rings."

I pulled out all the metal and put them in the cup tray between our seats. The darkness around the car welcomed me, calling like a siren. No others were on the road. We had the open highway to ourselves—trees and hills all around. Leaves blew with that soft *slinck* sound that they made when they'd gone hard and fragile. The farther from civilization we got, the stronger I felt. My trembling eased, my heartbeat steadied, but I was ready. I could almost feel the ground beneath my paws, earth pulsing through me.

"Shit, Sei." Gabe jerked the car off the road, parked, and turned the lights off. He sounded so far away, but he leaned across and opened the door. He tugged a cloth away from me, part of the human life I'd already forgotten. I jumped out, four paws instead of two legs, and I ran for the trees.

For a few seconds it felt like running from everything I was, until I shed that last bit of humanity and just let the earth pull me in the direction it wanted. The ground was starting to get cold, leaves falling from the trees and little things preparing for the winter. I loved the fall and all the secrets that began to unfold as winter set in. There would still be plenty to eat and warm places to sleep. I just needed to run for a while.

Somewhere among the fallen leaves of an ancient oak, I toyed with a mouse. Chased him from pile to pile and then off to his tiny hole in the ground, where I couldn't follow. An owl hooted above, warning me away from its prey, but I was the bigger predator tonight. A quick scurry up the tree brought me just branches from the obnoxious bird, which squawked and flew off.

Crunching of leaves, the sound of approaching footsteps

made the hairs on my neck rise. This one smelled of earth, but had the shape of a man. He'd been given back to the earth, only to break free from it. His eyes seemed to search the branches for me, but I was small and gray and could hide from some of the most dangerous predators.

"Sei?" He stepped closer to my tree, and I backed farther into the hollow between the upper branches. "I have a cabin nearby. If you follow my scent, you'll find it. I have to go. The sun will be up soon. Please follow. The road is close, and I want you to be safe."

He stared in my direction for a few more seconds before picking his way through the trees and off to the east. My brain in simplified cat form made normal things harder to recognize, but my instincts usually took good care of me.

Maybe the earthman had food. Sometimes humans put out dishes of tasty meat, free of bones and feathers. I waited until I was sure he was moving ahead before I hurried down and stealthily followed.

The earthman stood near an outcropping made of moss-covered rock. It looked like a tiny mountain jutting out of the ground and was surrounded by trees. He lifted a large rock and pushed it aside—revealing a hole—then crouched and disappeared inside. A light flickered on. I slunk back into a bush, waiting for him to come out. He stuck his head out, holding an odd, glowing stick in his hand.

"You coming? I have canned chicken at the cabin. The real stuff, not that crap made for pets."

He disappeared back into the hole, and I followed the bobbing light slowly, letting it get far enough ahead for my eyes to adjust to night vision. This place was some kind of tunnel. Long, damp, dark, and filled with mice. I chased a few. Teased and scared them, but let them run instead of eating them. The earthman paused each time I got distracted, waiting until I followed again. He put out his light halfway through and just sat down on a rock while I chased a large centipede. They had so many legs they were hypnotizing, even in the darkness. It wiggled from side to side, rowing one set of legs and then the other. I watched it dance for a time, even putting my paw next to it when it stopped to startle it back to movement. Sadly, it climbed too high for me to reach. Claws didn't work well on rocks.

The sun would rise soon. I felt it in my bones, which yawned and cracked in rumbled warning. I stretched and looked at the man. Did he still want me to follow? He got up and continued through the tunnel. We emerged in a dark heavily wooded area beside a stream. I leapt into the water to wash off the dust and bat at a few fish. Again the man waited, though the set of his shoulders was tight. The first glimmer of daylight was beginning to peek over the horizon. It would take some time to penetrate the trees, but the promise of it ran like ants crawling across my spine.

I turned and nipped at the man. Danger! Somehow I knew he'd be hurt if he stayed out in the light. He hurried ahead with me bouncing behind—ignoring snakes and rabbits—and swiping at his heels if he didn't move fast enough. Finally we came to a large den, human-style, of dark wood, surrounded by rocks, with trees growing out of it. He opened the door and motioned for me to get inside. Once we both were in, he closed the door and set a wooden bar in place. This darkness was deeper even than the tunnel, and I could hardly see him at all.

He lit the light stick again and set it in a high-up place. The space was several feet wide, but barely tall enough to fit his great height. Several different size shelves held bottles, cans, and tools. A ladder to his right led up to a tiny hole of darkness in the wall. I didn't much like the idea of the closed door blocking me in, but understood that it kept the sun out. Not that I was sure why that needed to be.

The man patiently opened a can and poured its contents onto a plate.

The smell was heavenly to my empty stomach. He set the plate on the floor beside me, and I wasted no time devouring the delicious meat. No feathers, no bones, no scales, just *yum*. I purred into the dish before I'd gotten halfway finished, and licked it clean.

The earthman took off his clothes, then pulled a few crinkling bags out of a large storage bin. He opened one and freed several huge, warm-looking blankets and stuffed them into the dark hole above the main open area. I jumped on the crinkle bag and chewed on its tasty, slippery surface until it made me sneeze.

"Jamie can't tell me what your interest in plastic is. It doesn't interest his bear at all. Maybe it's a cat thing. And I know it's an odd mix for you, remembering some human things, but forgetting others." He climbed up into the hole and wrapped the blankets around himself, leaving a small opening for me. "Coming in?"

The tingle of the sun warned me again, making a shudder run through my tired bones. I hadn't really done much tonight. Hadn't even caught a mouse or two. Why was I so tired? I leapt up into the space, inspected it for insects and happily found none, then settled between his body and the blankets. A full tummy and a warm space were all I really needed.

He slid a wooden plank over the opening of the hole and settled in. I curled nose to tail and purred while he stroked my fur in a familiar fashion. Sleep took me in the middle of that peace and comfort.

CHAPTER 7

The smell of bacon frying invaded my dreams sometime later. The overly sweet stench of syrup made my stomach turn. I opened my eyes to pure darkness and the feel of skin against mine and a blanket. Stretching out my now very human limbs, I let the sleepiness fade away.

Vague memories of last night settled in. The thought of the white room made my heart pound. Gabe didn't move beside me, but it was probably only around ten or so in the morning. Despite the darkness of our hiding place, I could feel the sun hanging low yet in the sky. Vampires slept an almost dead sleep during the daylight hours, though every one of them had a different amount of time they needed to rest. During that time they were helpless, which is why they often went back to their graves for safety.

This place didn't feel like a grave. The blankets were soft, and the scent of the grave dirt Gabe had under his bed was very faint. He obviously didn't stay here much.

A knock on the plank that separated us from the rest of the hut made me jump and bang my head on the low roof. "Ouch."

I pushed the wood back, wondering just who knew about this

place and had gotten in. Didn't surprise me at all to find it was Jamie. He smiled at me. "Want eggs and bacon or pancakes?"

"Eggs. And please put the syrup away. The smell makes me sick."

"Sure. Gabe said your nose is really sensitive, cat or not." He moved across the room to the tiny wood stove I hadn't noticed last night and capped the syrup, then flipped the bacon. "There's a duffel bag of your things on the table over there. You can go wash up in the stream if you want. Just be sure to close the upper panel before you open the door."

I jumped down, slid the plank back into place, grabbed the bag, and opened the door. Not being all that much of a camp-outside kind of guy, I hurried to relieve myself and washed off in the stream as best I could before pulling on a T-shirt and some jeans. The chilly days meant I was going to need something warmer if I stayed here much longer.

Finally feeling as clean as I could get without a bar of soap, I headed back inside. Jamie handed me a plate full of scrambled eggs and bacon.

"Kind of a heavy breakfast," I told him.

"Eat what you need."

"Do you have any fruit?" I ate a piece of bacon and started on the eggs. How many had he given me? Three, maybe four? And ten slices of bacon? I guess if I were a bear, I'd eat this much....

He dug into a bag that sat on the floor beside the door and offered me a banana and an apple. I took the banana. "Thanks."

His own plate was heaped full of twice as much food as mine. I really didn't know what else to say to him. What do you say to a coworker who watches you get arrested for murder?

"I called the university. Classes are canceled for today, but the school is open. Your mom scheduled your retest for Friday. And she's requiring you to go to a party Friday night. Something about eligible women? Aren't you gay?"

I groaned, reminded that I would have to be a sperm donor.

Did I really have to get to know the girls? Was I going to be expected to pay conjugal visits? "How did you get here, anyway? Are you Gabe's new vamp wannabe?"

Jamie shrugged. "Jealous he may want to bite someone else?"

"Yes," I answered honestly. Though I proclaimed I trusted and cared for no one, Gabe was someone I probably couldn't live without. Funny how he'd worked his way into my life and now I was kind of used to having him around.

The teasing look on Jamie's face vanished. "He's crazy about you. And I'm here for you, not him."

"Do you have to be so creepy all the time?" I pushed the rest of my food toward him and peeled the banana. He dumped all my leftovers on his plate and plowed through it.

"I don't know why you see protective as creepy. But it's not my place to change how you see the world. Just make it easier for you to live in it."

He always said such odd things. Most guys I could get a read on fairly quickly and knew how to push their buttons to get what I wanted, but Jamie was a mystery. "Why am I so important?" I had to ask.

"I would think with your past that being important to anyone would make you happy. And you are important to me and to Gabe."

"My past has taught me that people will pull the chair out from under you just when you think it's safe to sit down. Gabe will get bored of me eventually. And I don't get why you are such a hanger-on." I threw the banana peel into the bag of garbage hanging by the door and rubbed my arms. The little hut got cold fast.

Jamie got up, tugged off his hoodie, and handed it to me. "It's clean, I promise."

I took it, sniffed it out of habit, and because it didn't smell bad, yanked it over my head. Even three sizes too big, it was warm. "Thanks."

"You're welcome. If you're ready, we have a hike to get to the car."

I looked up to where Gabe slept. "We're leaving?"

"Your mom is insisting you make an appearance at school today. Go to the library or something. Just be seen on campus."

"Because people think I killed my teacher."

"No one thinks you killed her, Seiran. Someone pushed her through your wards. It could have happened to anyone. Tanaka made a statement about you being a victim of multiple attacks and this is just another attempt to discredit her. You won't even go to trial for the wards." Jamie cleaned up the stove and put everything away before gesturing me toward the door.

It was more than a little worrisome that my mom was pushing hard to erase something I very well could have done. Did she want a baby that bad? Or did she really believe me that I didn't kill the professor or Frank? "So people are supposed to think the professor's death happening the day after Frank was found dead on my doorstep is just a coincidence?"

"Are you saying you killed them?" He led a path through the woods in the opposite direction we'd come last night.

"Hell, no. I don't think I could kill anyone. Not even my mom, and I'm pretty sure she's gonna kill me someday. But it can't look good to the police."

"The police try to keep out of magic affairs. They let the Dominion handle all that. Andrew Roman wants you. You don't do him any good in jail—so he'll work things on his end too."

We emerged into a wooded parking area off the end of a dirt road. Gabe's car sat there, not Jamie's. I didn't remember us leaving the highway last night.

"Detective Roman seems to want me to burn."

"He wouldn't. You're exactly what he's been searching for, except for the whole being gay thing. I don't think he likes homosexuals. He likes Gabe even less, and you're involved with him, so maybe that's it too." Jamie climbed into the car, and I lumbered to the passenger side, feeling a lot heavier today than I normally did. It was probably the bacon.

"You make no sense. How am I what he's searching for?"

"He gave you his card, right?"

"Yeah." It was in the pocket of the pants I'd left at Gabe's place.

"Call him. Ask about the Ascendance. You'd make a great figurehead, maybe even have the ability to change the organization for the better." Jamie shrugged and started the car. We headed out of the wilderness, back toward civilization. "I'll drop you off at school and pick you up by the library around five. Stay close to the campus, please."

"Some babysitter you are." People around me were dying. The campus had a lot of students and that made for a lot of targets. Or maybe it was meant to make me a harder target to hit.

"I heard Gabe call you 'baby' once. You nearly bit his head off. I won't make the same mistake."

CHAPTER 8

On campus, I felt like even more of a freak show than I usually did. I didn't even have the clothes today to walk the walk and pretend it didn't bother me. I spent most of the day in the library, copying recipes from my favorite nutrition magazines. By the time my stomach growled, it was after 2:00 p.m.

I looked up to find Brock staring at me from across the library. He was sitting with the blond guy again, though the blond had his back to me, leaving Brock's curious expression in my direct line of sight—it was a little unnerving. This time I had no desire to smile. That didn't seem to deter him. He came and sat down across from me.

"Hi," he said.

"Hello, Brock. Shouldn't you be at practice or something?" Anywhere but here, staring at me like I was some kind of idol he couldn't wait to fuck.

"Canceled, like everything else. There are grief counselors set up everywhere, trying to get people to talk. The news said you were arrested."

"I was. But they got the wrong guy. So they let me go." I

flipped the pages of my magazine and found a recipe for cheese-stuffed peppers with almonds and cherry tomatoes.

"There's a party next weekend. We keep it quiet on campus. Invite only—"

"I don't think you and me party in the same circles." Brock set off my creep-meter about as much as Jamie did. Popular guys like him just didn't hang with guys like me. Not unless they wanted to screw me, and he did not seem the type. I remembered all too well my encounter with Ryan Federoff my freshman year. He'd been the first, but not the last. If I learned anything from my years on campus, it was to avoid the jocks.

He put his hand over mine, and I looked up to see his brown eyes pleading. "It's important. It's a secret group. We call ourselves Ascendance. It's for guys like us. Male witches."

Like the same Ascendance Jamie had said Detective Roman was a part of? "Where's the party?"

Brock smiled and let out a deep breath, then grabbed my pen and jotted an address down on the top of my recipe page in my notebook. "It's in Isanti, so it's a bit of a drive, but it will be fun. I promise. Starts at seven on Saturday, goes 'til whenever. It's a time to let loose. A lot of guys practice magic at these things. I've even seen a few change."

It sounded illegal as hell. "I may have to work. But I'll think about it."

He studied me a few minutes longer while I copied down more recipes and fished through more magazine pages. "You're hard to get a read on," he finally said.

Funny, 'cause usually no one cared enough to try. "I'm just not in the mood for conversation today. Sorry, Brock. Have a nice day." I gave him my best bar smile. He nodded, got up, and walked away.

When Jamie arrived at five, I had a notebook full of new recipes but no access to try them since my house was under quarantine.

Jamie picked me up in his car but drove me to Gabe's condo, riding the elevator down with me to the new basement apartment. Had it been only a day ago I'd come here for the first time, and practically run from the place in fear that Gabe was trying to trap me? Sure he did a lot of little things to make me more comfortable, but that was because he cared, right?

I didn't bother setting wards. Any idiot who broke into a vampire's home deserved to die. And a vampire would kill to protect its territory without much provocation.

The bathroom, with its fancy glass-surround shower, called my name. I stepped inside feeling unlike myself. Didn't even need to jack off under the hard spray. Instead I just let the water cleanse the past two days from me like shedding an old skin. By the time I stepped out and dried off, I had already decided how the night was going to go—depending on what Gabe had already stocked in the pantry I might need to go shopping.

An oversized T-shirt was all I wore as I headed for the kitchen. A note on the counter from Jamie said that he'd gone to get Gabe and would be back soon. Whatever. After the close of a new moon, I rarely wanted to be around people. So the empty condo was soothing.

I spread my notebook of recipes out on the wide granite countertop and shifted through them until I found the one I'd been contemplating earlier. The pantry was as well-stocked as I'd kept my own kitchen. In fact, the pots and knives were all the exact brand and style I used. That seemed more like Jamie's stalking observance than Gabe pushing me to commit. I shrugged it off, like everything else, and put myself to work. Not like I had anywhere else to be, other than maybe the bar. And I always had the day following the new moon off to recover. Eventually I'd sleep, and it would be a long, dead sleep.

By the time the door opened and voices filled the apartment, I'd finished most of the cooking and begun to doze on a chaise near the kitchen. Cinnamon and sugar scented the apartment.

Thankfully there were two ovens, since I'd made half a dozen dishes. Most of them were covered and ready to be cooked, but put in the fridge 'til later. The pie had been a last-minute thought, since I had almond flour and wheat germ already out for a crust on the tilapia I'd found in the fridge. The crisp apples and tart cranberries smelled heavenly, baking in a simple sugar and cinnamon mix.

"It smells amazing in here. What are you cooking?" Jamie asked.

Gabe glanced my way and briefly flashed me his beautiful smile before heading to the bedroom.

I yawned and stretched. "Stuffed green peppers with almonds, gouda, and cherry tomatoes. There's black-walnut bread cooling by the stove and a cranberry apple pie, which is almost done." The timer on the microwave said ten minutes. "There's also cilantro-lime wild rice in the cooker." I'd made a lot in case Jamie was staying. If not, I'd have leftovers.

Jamie leaned over the rice cooker and opened the lid. Steam poured out at him as he took a deep breath. "So good! I don't have your keen sense of smell, but I can smell the pie. And this rice looks delicious." He flicked the oven light on and looked at the peppers. "You made a lot of food."

"It's what he does when he's stressed," Gabe said from the doorway to his bedroom. He'd changed clothes and looked ready for work. He crossed the room and kissed me lightly on the lips. "There's an organic food site that delivers—even in the middle of the night. It's bookmarked on the computer. So if there's something you need but don't have, just add it to my account. Don't go out, except with Jamie. It's not safe."

"Okay," I told him. It was all a little overly domestic for me— me cooking and him going off to be the breadwinner. Not that I would ever let him financially support me. If being the son of Tanaka Rou had taught me anything, it was that I had to work for what I wanted and take nothing from anyone.

I got up and went to check on the peppers, moving around Jamie to grab the oven mitt. The cheese bubbled around the edges, so I pulled them out and set them on the cooling rack. Gabe was putting on his shoes. "You working tonight?" I really didn't want to be alone though I'd been craving solitude before they showed up. Yeah, my brain was pretty fucked up.

"Yes. You'll be sleeping soon. Jamie will stay here with you. I have cable and a bunch of movies. And you have a pantry of supplies that will keep you busy until you drop off." He didn't need to warn me away from Jamie tonight. I was too tired—both physically and emotionally—to do anything. "And Jamie can make sure all the appliances are off so you don't set the place on fire."

"I've never—"

"You killed my toaster oven upstairs. Remember, sprinklers went off and everything?"

I sighed and turned off both ovens. The pie would finish just fine in the lasting warmth. I pulled the knife and cutting board out and lifted the bread free of its cooling wrap to slice it. Everything here was stored the same place as my kitchen. Now it wasn't creepy, it was just comforting—especially since I didn't have that kitchen anymore. I'd probably never get my deposit back. I wondered if there were any similar buildings with basement apartments near the outskirts of the city.

"When do you think I'll be able to go get my stuff?"

"I'm sure they've dusted everything, vacuumed the floor eight times, and torn apart every drawer looking for clues. Call the police station tomorrow and ask."

The thought of people in my house, moving my things, making a mess made me shiver. I immediately went to scrubbing Gabe's counter to make sure it was as spotless after my adventure in cooking as my own kitchen would be.

"What's your deal with Detective Roman, anyway? Is he an old lover or something?"

Gabe just shook his head. "No deal." He swung on his coat and crossed the room to lean over the counter to kiss me on the cheek. Again so domestic, I froze. He laughed and headed for the door, calling to Jamie. "If there's an issue…."

"I know," Jamie replied.

The door opened and closed. Alone with Jamie again. "Hungry?" I asked him.

"You'll let me eat some of that?"

"I certainly can't eat it all."

I pulled out a few plates, handed him one, and dished a pepper and a bowl of rice for myself. A couple of slices of fresh bread with a dab of sweet cream butter, and I was set. "Eat as much as you want."

Jamie waited until I moved to sit at the tiny two-seater table before dishing a plate full of three stuffed peppers, a heaping bowl of rice, and a stack of bread. He sat across from me at the little table. I took a bite of the pepper. It was good, but missing something. I looked toward the kitchen.

"No wine fridge?" I wondered out loud.

"He's got cool storage at the back of the pantry. Maybe there?"

I headed into the walk-in pantry and flicked on the light, trying not to wonder how Jamie knew so much about Gabe's new place. The handle at the back of the room was the only marker of the door. I pulled it open and peered inside. Cold storage, indeed. No large slabs of meat, but lots of fruits and vegetables and a rack full of wine. I chose a dry white and headed back to the table.

Jamie had already set out the glasses. "Does Gabe drink with you sometimes? I know he can drink natural fluids."

"Yeah. But only when he knows he won't be drinking my blood. Then it's just a double whammy. Drunk vampire."

"Really? That I'd like to see."

"Hmm" was all I said. Gabe got really sappy when he was drunk. Spewed lots of L words and sweet things that would have most people sighing heavenly in adoration. It made me feel weird, so I never liked him drunk around me and he avoided it when he could.

I dug into my pepper. The melted cheese, sweet tomatoes, and crunchy almonds made me nearly giddy. With the bite of the wine, by the time I was done, I was not only sleepy, but satisfied as well. I rinsed my plate before putting it in the dishwasher and took the pie out of the oven to cool.

"You're an amazing cook. You should have your own restaurant."

"I wanted to." A long time ago, back when I was into fitness and thought I got to choose my own path in life.

"But your mom didn't want you to?"

"She wants me to stick with the magic. Carry on the Rou line."

"You can't be a professional chef and an earth witch at the same time?"

I shrugged and headed to the bedroom. All the health guides said to wait two hours after a meal before sleeping, but none of them talked about the night after a new moon set. I brushed my teeth in a hurry and headed to bed. Gabe had changed the sheets again for me. I snuggled into them and wrapped myself around his pillow.

Jamie moved around in the kitchen. I heard the water run and then the clink of his dishes going into the washer. I must have been tired if I forgot to clean those. He came into the room and stood in the doorway, staring at me. "Are you going to sleep now?"

"I'll doze off in a while, I'm sure." I felt sleepy, but sometimes I just couldn't get my brain to turn off. "I should double-check to make sure the ovens are off."

"They're off." He crossed the room and went into the bathroom. The shower turned on. I began to doze again just as I heard the water turn off. He came out in a towel, went to the closet and dug through Gabe's side until he found a pair of boxers and slid into them. Then he left the room. I closed my eyes and tried to stop worrying about the week to come so sleep would take me.

The apartment got very dark. I opened my eyes again.

All the lights were off. "Jamie?"

"Yeah?" His voice came from somewhere close to the room.

"Can you leave a light on, please? Just one."

"Okay." The lamp on the far side of the kitchen went on. He came back and closed the bedroom door all but a tiny bit.

"Thank you."

"You're welcome."

I dozed for a while, just on the edge of sleep but still half-awake, and heard Jamie talking quietly on the phone to someone. After a while he was quiet, but I felt something startle me awake and looked up to see him staring at me. "See? Creepy," I mumbled.

He laughed lightly. "You want company of the nonsexual kind?"

I shrugged and rolled over, making room for him. He crawled in and pulled the blanket up around his shoulders before turning to face away from me. "Who were you talking to?" I asked.

"My mom."

Big strong bear-of-a-guy Jamie? "You get along okay?"

"Better than you and your mom, I suspect. She's pretty supportive of me. About most things at least."

"She knows you're an earth witch?" An earth witch almost as strong as I was.

"Both my mom and dad are/were earth witches."

"Your dad?"

"He passed away. A long time ago."

"I'm sorry."

"It's okay. He died shortly before you were born. So it's been a really long time." He sounded sad, though.

I didn't know what to say for a while. Bringing up that I didn't even know who my dad was didn't seem like a good idea. Finally

I said, "Sorry if you're ever hurt by what I say. I sorta just say things that pop in my head."

"Yeah. I've noticed that about you. At first it bugged me. You'd get this disgusted look on your face when I was around. I finally asked Gabe, and he told me a few things."

"Like what?"

"Your verbal diarrhea was the first thing he told me about. You say whatever you think. He told me about your sensitive nose and the time when the two of you first met. You had known him less than five minutes when you asked him to fuck you."

I shrugged and snuggled further into the blankets. Jamie was like a furnace, and the heat pouring off him kept my feet from freezing. "He's hot. What can I say?"

"You were sixteen. Damn near blackmailed him into having sex with you that night." Jamie turned around and stared through the dark at me. The dim light of the room made it hard to read his expression.

"He wasn't my first. Far from."

Jamie sighed, long and heavy. "I really don't want to know. Anyway. Only after he hired me to work the bar did he tell me more stuff, like your OCD for cleaning."

"I'm not OCD."

"How many times did you clean the kitchen while you were cooking?"

"I don't know." I really didn't keep track.

"After you took out or put away any new ingredient?"

"I like a clean kitchen when I cook," I protested.

"And how many times do you have to check to be sure the oven is off?" When I didn't answer, Jamie's rumbling laughter made me smack him in the chest. Not that it mattered. It probably felt like a mosquito bite to him.

"If you think I'm so weird, why are you stalking me?"

"I don't think you're weird. And I'm stalking you, as you put it, because I love you."

I raised myself up on an elbow to stare at him. "That's a hell of a confession, seeing as how we're in bed together."

"Not *in love* with you. Love you. *Gabe* is in love with you. Even though you're a pain in the ass to him. And *you* are in love with Gabe, no matter how much you deny it. I love you. That's it. No bells or singing angels."

I lay back down and wondered at the smooth expanse of the ceiling. "I'm all messed up inside, you know. Bad core, and all that."

"You think you're not worthy of anyone loving you. That's your mother's doing. Parents should take care of their children. Show you that even when life's tough, they are there to give you a hug. But it's okay. I can work with it, messed-up insides or not. You should get some rest."

"Your mom is like that?"

"She is now. She wasn't always. Before my dad died, she was mean, like your mom."

"Did she love your dad?"

"No. But she loved me. It took my dad's death for her to realize that."

"I'm sorry."

"Sleep. You need rest."

I sighed, bunched up my pillow, and closed my eyes. Sleep finally arrived.

CHAPTER 9

The next day was back to business as usual. I got up feeling refreshed and went to class. Brock and I walked around campus together. He waited outside of class when I was finished and followed me to the next. No one dared to stare long while he lingered. I'd never had a school friend who actually treated me like something more than a quick fuck. It was kind of nice. Sometimes he looked at me like that was what he was thinking—wondering what it would be like to screw me—but he never made an advance and I wanted to keep it that way.

He talked about classes he would take next semester, one of them being Intro to Magic 101. It was a freshman class, but apparently a lot of guys were now trying to get their foot in the magic door. He didn't have to be accepted into the Magic Studies program to take the class, but anyone in the MS program had to take it. If Andrew Roman was inspiring the movement, I guess he couldn't be all bad.

After an early dinner of crusted tilapia and leftover rice from last night, I got ready for work. Gabe had tried to give me the day off, but I refused. I'd need money even more now to put down a new deposit—if anyone would be willing to rent to a male witch again.

I pulled up to the bar at a quarter to seven, ready for the long evening and dressed like my normal self. Mike was behind the bar again. No Gabe. Jamie appeared to be working both the bar and the tables. It was oddly busy for a Tuesday night. Thankfully, it was all the regulars tonight: Jack in his spot at the bar, Betsy and Lara in a booth, and Jo sitting at a two-seater table by herself, crying into her beer.

Shit. I'd forgotten about Frank. Had I missed the funeral?

I grabbed my apron from the back before heading to Jo's table and gave Jamie a nod in her direction. He shrugged and continued the frenzied pace. I sat down across from Jo and offered her a fresh napkin for her tears.

"I'm sorry, Joey," I told her quietly. Some friend I was, not calling or anything after her boyfriend died. Had she and Frank been exclusive?

She glanced at me and burst into heavier tears. "Seiran...." Her voice got all whiny and high-pitched. I winced when she grabbed my hand with a death grip. "You're a nice boy. You shouldn't work here. You'll die too, just like Frank and the professor."

"I'll be okay, Joey. Gabe won't let trouble stick around here long. If he finds that serial killer, the guy better run the other way."

Jo shook her head. "There will be trouble until everything is balanced again. They've been saying that for decades. Ever since they killed John Ruffman in the sixties." Ruffman had led a cult of male witches whose power rivaled the Dominion. Every one of them who'd been caught had been burned, including Ruffman. "Ruffman said balance was the key. But everything is so...." She searched for the word, eyes wide.

"Out of sync?" I asked, not sure where this conversation was going.

She grabbed both my hands. "You should be like Ruffman, Seiran."

"Oh hell no. I am not burning."

"Not that part. You're a Rou. You can make the Dominion listen. You're a strong earth witch. Show them your power. You could be Pillar. You could give us back our equilibrium."

That was a big word for a very drunk woman. "There are plenty of other, more powerful witches out there."

"But none of them have a good heart, like you." She looked so sappy when she said it, I couldn't help but laugh.

"Don't ruin my street cred, J."

"You joke, but it's true."

I pulled her up from her seat and put a twenty on the table. I caught Mike's eye and let him know I was taking Jo home. He nodded and waved me off. Jo swayed unsteadily on her feet as I guided us to my car. She'd have to take a cab back tomorrow for hers, but at least she'd get home safely. After strapping her in the passenger seat, I paused and looked back at the bar. Gabe and Jamie would have a fit if I left. But it wasn't like I expected either of them to babysit me forever. In fact, it really annoyed me.

Sighing in frustration, I sent Gabe a text message, telling him where I was going and that it wouldn't take long. Then I got in the car and headed toward Jo's apartment in St. Paul.

"I'm not strong enough of an earth witch for you, Seiran" was the first thing she said during the drive. We'd gotten halfway to her place with nothing but the radio singing between us.

"I don't know what you mean."

"Your mom has called all eligible earth witches, level three or higher, to a party on Friday for you. I'm only a level two."

Shit. The baby thing again. "You don't want to be a baby maker, Jo. You don't want my mom breathing fire down your neck to have a girl or die trying. Be happy you don't fit the bill."

"But you're going to have babies. Frank and I won't ever have babies now."

Frank should never have had babies anyway. But thankfully, my censor was on today, and I kept my mouth shut.

"You'll make strong babies. The whole of the Dominion is talking about it. The Ascendance too. They both want you for the same thing. Neither thinks they can control you, so they want a child they *can* control, with your kind of power."

I hit the brake so fast we were almost rear-ended. What the fuck? I pulled into an empty lot at Savers and turned to her. "What the hell are you talking about? I thought the Ascendance was supposed to be some kind of secret."

Jo laughed bitterly. "There are thousands of men joining every day. The Dominion may be old-fashioned, but they aren't stupid. And you are the poster boy for earth power at the moment. Ruffman was, long ago, but he died too easily. You would be one hell of a fight. Lycans are attracted to you. One of the most powerful vampires in North America worships the ground you walk on. My mom talked about you on the phone with another council member when you got arrested Sunday night."

"They were talking about killing me?" My blood went cold. Was this why Jamie and Gabe stuck so close to me? Did they know the Dominion had finally had enough?

"It's not the first time. They've told Tanaka for years to put a leash on you so you wouldn't end up with the Ascendance. I remember talking to my mom once, after you started at the bar, about how nice you really were. She said it was all an act that you put on so the Dominion didn't come for you."

I rested my head against the steering wheel, not looking at her, not wanting to think about what it meant. Professor Cokota's murder should have meant my death. Yet they had stopped. My mother had insisted they stop when I'd been certain my entire life that she'd be the first to call for my death.

Why?

Because there was no female heir to inherit my power.

If I had a child, they could perform an inheritance ceremony before they lit me on fire and gave all my power to the baby upon my death. Which meant the second my child was conceived, the clock would begin ticking.

I suddenly felt very sick. They were going to do it this time, weren't they? How could I really mean so little to anyone? Had Gabe known? Would he still have insisted that I have a child just to be free of my mother for a few hours when she was going to kill me anyway?

Swallowing back the bile, I pulled out of the lot and took Jo home, ignoring her other statements but promising to call. I didn't even bother returning to the bar. I just drove.

The world lost its grip and clarity around me while I roared down that long, dark highway away from the Cities, away from everything I knew. Was there a place that I could run far enough away to be free from the Dominion?

Nothing mattered while I rolled down that dark path to nowhere. Following 35 south, the space between towns grew longer and longer. My cell phone rang, but I ignored it. The overwhelming feeling of defeat reminded me of my first year in college as the only guy studying magic. Everyone had taken to picking on me. The jocks pushed me around, stole my books, and took the wheels off my car, more than once. Girls gave me dirty looks and whispered loudly about me.

The many times my room had been vandalized stuck out as the worst. I'd had an Asian Ball Joint Doll, one so few people had. Only fifty in the world, and I'd saved up for three years, working part-time jobs in high school to pay for it. I found it broken into tiny little pieces. The hard resin wouldn't have been easy to break, so someone had really worked at it. I packed up my things, including the scattered pieces of that pretty doll, and moved out of the dorms. Leaving school hadn't been an option—I never wanted to return to my mother's terrible white room. But even moving out of the dorms hadn't made life easier.

I learned quickly to date outside the school that year. Two

attempted rapes proved to me it was better to be outdoors if I was with anyone I didn't trust completely.

The older I got, the more the earth responded. I went from not having to change at all on the new moon to needing to almost all three nights. The earth turned in a power-filled pool of energy that always seemed to cycle through me.

Gabe and I grew closer, but I couldn't expect more. No one needed the messed-up creature I'd become. He gave me as much freedom as I wanted and still helped me maintain a home by paying me well and putting up with my eccentricity. I loved the bar, and Gabe had been a rock in my life while I was the sand flowing around him trying to get him to move.

For four years I'd let people glare at me. Four years of teasing, bullying, and hate-filled words. For what? To be a sperm donor and a smokestack? What was the point? Even Gabe couldn't get me out of that. If the Dominion wanted me dead, then I was dead.

Signs welcoming me to Iowa passed, and I ignored them, like everything else. Had to refill gas just over the border, but even that was done on autopilot. Not that I thought driving would solve anything or that I could escape the Dominion. They had two million members worldwide. Maybe more when it came to people who respected them and expected them to take care of rogues like me.

The night had long since grown dark, and the sliver of the moon lingered overhead before I pulled the car off the road and followed a dirt path for a while. No idea where I was, or even what I was going to do. But when I parked the car and got out, I wanted nothing to do with the corruption of the world. I just wanted to be free of all the troubles humanity brought.

Changing on nights other than the new moon would have been impossible for a lower-level witch. For me, it was an hour of nearly endless pain. I felt every muscle stretch and collapse, bones break and reform, fur emerge from sensitive flesh. When the change was finally done, I lay panting, letting the pure power of the earth flow through me. The waves of power lapped at all my troubles like a tide washing away a shore, until much of the humanity disappeared inside me.

I must have napped for a while, because when I awoke it was early and the sun was starting to rise in the distance. The stink of the car made me move away from it and into the spread of the land. Trees grouped here and there. Fields of tall stalks smelled of humans, and I wanted none of that.

Hunting rabbits and chasing mice filled the time as night pressed into day. I kept moving, napping when I got tired, hunting when I was hungry. Nothing else mattered. The day passed to night, and I found my way to a thick, unscarred bit of land that smelled of deer, coyotes, and wild turkey. Open space. The earth pulsed strong here, unbroken by human hands.

I wound my way through this new place, thinking it could be home. A happy stream burbled a clean flow of fresh water. Lapping it soothed my dry mouth. I found a hollow high up on a big pine tree that would make a nice, safe refuge away from the few larger predators who would find me tasty. An abandoned nest inside was years old, and I shoved it out to clean my den before curling up to bathe away all the dust of the days past. The air grew colder, and the ground told me a storm was coming, rain probably, cold and fast. In my little hole, I tucked in my short tail and purred myself to sleep.

The rush of rain didn't bother my dry hollow. It was almost soothing, the sound of the rain tapping against the tree and dripping off the leaves. After the downpour slowed came a silence that made my ears twist forward. No crickets, no birds, just the wind. Either there was a very nasty storm coming, or something dangerous moved through the trees.

I opened my mouth to pull in a deep breath and circle it around to taste the air. Pine was the strongest scent, but underneath… something bitter and rank. Something that made my fur stand on end. I peered through the branches to the ground below and watched the large shape move. It was dark brown in color and about fifteen times my size. One of my few fears: a bear.

Just my luck. Find a nice, peaceful home with lots of rabbits and tasty little birds only to stumble into the territory of an anti-social earth-pig. They were terrible—like humans, taking up so much space, slumbering half the year in their smelly dens, and always stealing my food for their babies.

I eased out onto one of the higher branches, digging my claws in for added grip. The air wasn't rank with the stench of more bears. Just this one. And he didn't smell like the normal sort of bear.

The bear stood up on his back legs and let out a mild grunt before putting his nose to the earth again. He ambled toward my tree, and I stood, ready to hold my ground. No way was that big bear going to fit in my little tree home. He passed close enough to my tree to make me hiss and arch my back at him.

He paused, looked directly at me, and backed away from the tree. Sitting on his back legs, he looked like an overgrown prairie dog. I liked prairie dogs. They were fun to chase and had a lot more meat than a mouse. But this overgrown mouse wannabe wasn't getting my tree. I hissed at him again. He just waited.

Then I heard the soft crunch of leaves in an unmistakable sound. Human feet. Usually clumsier, heavier than these, but these were similar. Then came the heartbeat. Slower than mine or the bear's. No normal human approached a bear without his heart racing. Yet this one was calm.

Finally, he stepped close enough that I could see him beyond all the branches of thick pine needles. He stood beside the bear. His clothes looked ragged, shoulders slumped. In his hand was a large box.

I flinched and backed toward my den. The box had holes in the side and bars on the front. *Cage*, came the memory from somewhere in the back of my mind. The man took a step forward, and I bolted into my hole. They'd have to take the tree down to get to me. No human was putting me in a cage.

I curled up far enough inside to watch the hole from a decent distance and waited. Time passed as the wind howled. The cold whipping of the rain returned, but none of the crickets or the birds did. The smell of bear still lingered close. And the human. An odd human. Familiar. But I associated it all with pain now and kept pushing it away. Until the branches in front of my new home cracked away and the human was there.

He stared at me, an unhappy look on his face, and reached inside. I tore the hell out of his hand—biting, scratching, and tearing into his soft flesh. He gripped the scruff of my neck and pulled, dragging me toward the only exit to my hovel. I yowled and clawed at his arm and the inside of the tree until he grasped me in a tighter hold, and I wilted like jelly in his hand. Once free of the tree, I noticed we seemed to be floating. The thought should have been alarming, but a second man stood below, holding open the cage.

The fight poured back into me. I clawed and hissed and growled. The man who held me bled but said nothing. He smelled of earth and sadness. I just wanted to be free and go back to chasing rabbits in my new home. They shoved me in the cage, then closed and bolted the door. Whatever they said was lost on me since they spoke in that strange foreign language humans had. The second man shivered but picked up the cage. The first man shook his head and reached for the box, taking it in his bleeding hand.

The blood dripped down his arm and onto me. I licked it away each time and hissed at him. The men moved in unison toward the edge of the peaceful land. The swaying of the cage began to make me nauseous. The taste of the man's blood was bitter and cold, not warm like the little things I often ate. It soon stopped dripping on me, and I rolled up in the back of the cage, trying to cushion myself from the constant bouncing.

The bite of tar and unnatural fluids came in a stink that made me sneeze. The two men got in a large box I vaguely recognized as a car. The earthman sat in the back on a long seat with me. The other one sat in a different seat and did something that made the car erupt with noise, and it began to move, making my sickness worse.

They kept speaking that odd language. The first man pulled out a little can and pried off the lid. The smell hit me in a wave of happiness and illness. He poured a little through the bars of my cage. Sweet meat. So tasty, even my nauseous tummy couldn't resist. The man touched my head through the bars, rubbing my ears and eyebrows, even though I bit him each time. He offered me more meat, until I ate and he could pet me without incident.

When the meat ran out, I retreated to the back of the box. He spoke in soothing tones that made no sense, other than the softness of his voice. I couldn't make out much of what he said, just pieces, "Love you," and "worried you were lost." He sighed heavily and sunk farther down into the seat, fingers still curled in my fur. "I know it's hard...."

I listened, trying to tune out the noise from the car. Gradually the sounds came together in my mind, forming words, though I didn't understand them all.

"I've downloaded a half-dozen new romances and put them on your reader. Even a few about shape shifters, since I know they interest you, though you are very different from any shifter I've ever met. A shifter would never be able to return to full human form after this long changed. I think your ability to stay and change at will proves that shifters are more biology than magic."

I moved in the cage to sit close to the bars and look up at him. He slouched in the seat, his body turned my way, eyes looking like dark summer grass. His fingers scratched under my chin, and I fought not to purr for him.

"There's more meat, but I think we'll wait until you're home.

Don't want to make you sick. Maybe we can get you to change back soon. I'd like to talk to you, something a little more two-sided than we have right now. Jo said you were very upset, and I think you ran because you have realized the severity of the situation. You need to understand that I'm not going to let anyone hurt you. You belong to me, Seiran Rou. And I belong to you."

After a while, he said, "Do you remember when we first met? That Halloween party out in the sticks of Wisconsin? You were dressed as a black cat. Tight leotard, tail, and headband for ears. I was a vampire, Vlad coat and all that lameness. You laughed at me but flirted like no one ever had before. You leaned in close, smelling so young, male, and sexy. I knew you were trouble. There was no doubting you wanted me. Not in that leotard. But you were so young. Sixteen, you told me later. You were so mad when I turned you down! Then you flirted with that lycan...."

His tone changed, sounding angry now. "He liked kids. Wanted you simply because you looked so young. The thought of him touching you still makes me want to rip him apart." He paused, and the tone calmed again. "Remember how I pulled him away from you and insisted that I take you home? You raged at me half the drive and tried to give me a blow job more than once. I wouldn't give in."

He sighed heavily. "Then you called me, a week before your seventeenth birthday. Not sure how you even got my number. But you demanded that I take you on a date, since you'd be legal." He rubbed my head again. "I shouldn't have agreed. I hadn't forgotten about you, the way you smelled like honey lemonade and how you looked in that leotard. I wanted you as bad as you wanted me. We never even made it to the movie. I wouldn't fuck you, and you whined that you didn't need the foreplay."

He moved in his seat again, staring out the window for a few seconds before resuming his endless petting of me. "We made love in the front seat of my car—you called it just a hand job— and you hated to call it love. Even then you were a player, so afraid someone would love you that you did everything you could to push everyone away. Matthew really did a number on you."

The man growled in frustration. The sound echoed around the backseat. I cringed and hoped the anger in his tone wasn't directed at me. "Matthew shouldn't have touched you. He was a predator. You were still a kid. I think if you'd never met him, you'd be okay. No OCD, anxiety, or trust issues. You have no idea how much it pisses me off that I have to clean up his mess."

His hand was a little rough when he brought it back down to scratch my ears again. I nipped at him, and he returned to the gentle rubbing of my head.

"We're almost home," the other man said from the front seat.

The man closest to me—Gabe was his name; I remembered now—ran his hands through his hair. His green eyes looked so tired. "You and me are in the same place, kitten. Nowhere to go, lost faith in the world, wanting to escape it all. But I love you, and that's what keeps me here. That and hope that someday you'll admit you love me back." I curled up around the hand he'd worked through the bars and purred against him. Gabe's voice always gave me added clarity, though I couldn't remember why. Maybe because he spent a lot of time with me, or 'cause he liked to rub my head and scratch my chin. Either way, his voice and touch were soothing.

"He does love you," the man from the front seat said. "His mom just messed him up."

"It wasn't just his mom. Remind me to tell you about his early college years."

"And then there was Matthew, right? How old was Sei?"

"Eleven." Gabe scratched my chin just right. And it was so good I had to scratch my left ear. He waited until I finished before rubbing my cheeks and head again. I liked that he smelled like me now.

"Shit."

"Yeah. Did you call Dr. Moler?"

"She'll be waiting for us at your place. Sei won't take drugs—you know that," The man driving said.

"Hmm." Gabe used his free hand to rub my ears again. Maybe he'd be a good owner. I could be a happy house cat, even if I was a little too big to sit on his lap. "Can you force the change if he refuses, Jamie? I really don't want to lose him to this."

"I can try. You're more likely to get him to change by commanding him."

"He'd never forgive me. Even if it was for his own good."

"Damn. Up a creek."

"That's for sure." The voices faded away to silence for the rest of the drive.

CHAPTER 10

The city looked familiar though still dark in the early hours of the morning and made my heart race. Gabe still petted me, as if hours of soothing couldn't wear him out. We pulled into a parking garage that stank of car fluid and cement. I sneezed several times while they parked and took me from the garage to a box that moved and then to a big, open space. Once the door was closed, Gabe set the cage on the floor and opened the barred box.

Hesitantly, I stepped out. The floor was hard and unnatural beneath my padded toes. Smelled that way too. A woman leaned against the counter. White coat and long red hair. She made no attempt to move toward me, and in fact hardly seemed to move at all. I crept, hunched low to the ground, ready to sprint and flee, though there seemed no exit to this cement-covered world. The smell of dirt drew me from somewhere far off to the right.

"Did you open the box?" Gabe asked.

"Yes. He already seems drawn to it. I thought you were joking. But he's really done a full change and held it." The woman sounded surprised.

An open doorway that led to the smell I sought made me slink faster. Inside the room, a large box filled with dirt beckoned like a chunky rabbit would after a long nap. After jumping in, I pushed the dirt around and rolled twice before curling up in the corner. Gabe knelt beside the box. He felt like the earth now. I wanted to roll in him and wrap my very being around him, so I curled around his arm and licked him like I really wanted to.

He laughed. "Don't get all excited on me. You'll have to change for that. Kitty form is nice for an afternoon with a good book with a cat on the lap, but not for sweaty man-sex."

I meowed at him, though it sounded more like a minor roar. He just raised a brow my way. I shook my tail and leapt at him, batting at his arm, which hung over the side and still looked torn up from earlier. The jagged marks peppered his arm like battle scars. The earthy taste made me calmer as I licked him.

"Do you want us to go?" the other man asked from the doorway.

"No. When he changes, he'll be too tired to do anything. And I want the doctor to look at him," Gabe answered.

"Let her look at your arm. He got you pretty good."

"It will heal." He smiled at the other man. "Have that frozen pie I asked you to buy?"

"Yep."

"Put it in the oven on broil."

"You want it to burn?"

Gabe nodded.

The doctor stepped up behind the other man. "I have an idea as well. You're positive about his OCD?"

"Yes. Whatever you think will help," Gabe said. She left the room. I licked Gabe, and he petted me. Things were nice until the smell of something burning hit my sensitive nose like a glass door in the way of a rabbit chase. Then a high-pitched beeping went off. I arched my back, folding my ears against my head, and glared through the open door. Gabe shrugged but moved aside far enough for me to jump out of the box. My feet hit the hard floor, and I licked each quickly, trying not to breathe in the terrible burning smell.

The other man pulled something black from the oven, and smoke billowed around him. He clicked the oven off and put the charred thing on the stovetop. At least the beeping had stopped. I stepped into the kitchen, only to put a paw right into white powder. I picked up the tainted foot and licked it. The terribly bland taste of white flour hit me. And it was everywhere! The floor… the counter…. Sticky handprints dotted the fridge and cabinet doors. I sneezed and wheezed at the awful sight. My heart pounded fast, and the change poured over me, forcing me back at a painfully fast rate.

Gabe wrapped his arms around me, helping me through the change with soft words. I wept at the mess of the kitchen. I wanted so badly to start cleaning. Shivering and tired, I clung to him. He carried me to the shower, stripped out of his clothes, and washed me gently, massaging my head while he shampooed my hair and kept skin to skin at all times.

"I need to clean the kitchen," I told him.

"Later."

"But I have to do it now."

"You have other, more painful things you're hiding from right now." And just like that, all the pain came back. Knowing the Dominion would kill me after I had a child and that the trouble I'd suffered in school had been for nothing. I wanted so badly to go back to the simple form of a lynx, live out my shortened life away from all humanity. Each time I thought to change again, Gabe would kiss me. Full-on lips, tongue, teeth, a fierce kiss that should have brought lust, but I was just too tired. When he finally shut off the water, I still shivered in his arms.

As soon as I was dry, he helped me into a robe and led me through the bedroom toward the kitchen. Instead of the horrible mess I remembered, it was now spotless. Jamie and the doctor stood on the other side of the counter, each with a bottle of spray cleaner and a rag in hand.

"But—" I whispered, feeling confused and so tired all at once. At least the shaking had stopped. Tentatively, I touched the counter. It was clean and gleamed under the pendant lights. The smell of the burned pie still hovered, but not nearly as strong. Gabe led me to the chaise, and I sat down. The woman stepped closer.

"Let her look you over, okay? You were changed for three days. I was afraid we'd never find you." Gabe's voice was still soothing in my ear, and I was so very tired.

The woman knelt beside the chaise. "I'm just going to check some of your vitals, Seiran. Okay?"

Since she said my name right, I nodded and let her prod me, look in my eyes, listen to my heart, and check me for injuries. Other than being overwhelmingly tired, I felt fine. But Gabe had yet to let go. He sat beside me, and while the doctor asked me questions, I laid my head on his chest, listening to his heartbeat. My first-year science teacher had talked about vampire hearts and how they beat at about half of normal human speed. His was just a calming rhythm in my ear.

The doctor shook my arm gently. My eyelids were so heavy as I tried to look at her that I just glanced her way. "I'm prescribing some antianxiety medication, Seiran. We'll start with a low dose. It should help with your OCD."

"I don't want drugs."

"Do you want to run away again if it means never seeing Gabe again?"

"He'll come for me," I mumbled. "He's my best friend."

"And your lover," she said.

"Sometimes."

"Why don't you want it to be all the time?" The doctor asked.

"Because no one who's with me all the time loves me. No one can handle the real me."

She seemed to think then said,. "I see. Will you take the drugs if I promise to check back in a couple of weeks once this is all over to see if you still need them?"

"I don't like unnatural things in my body. They make me funny."

She was silent for a few minutes, or maybe I dozed off. Then I heard, "All right. There's a more natural herb you can take. And adding a few things to your diet might help. I'll give Gabe the details, and he can tell you tomorrow."

"Okay," I whispered and let the total strength of unconsciousness take me away.

CHAPTER 11

The sleep seemed to have cleared my head, because I woke feeling stronger and more focused. Though there were no windows to show me the sunlight, I felt it. The earth awoke and told me it was time to get out of bed. Being wrapped around Gabe felt better than it should have. He was warm—rather than cold—and he stirred only a little when I got up and found my way to the shower. After the last of the sleepiness was washed away, I pulled on some sweats and one of Gabe's large T-shirts and headed to the kitchen.

The memory of the mess last night had me cleaning counter-tops and sweeping the floor again when Jamie walked in. He had a couple of grocery bags in hand and a duffel bag slung over his shoulder.

"Morning," I said, watching the coffeemaker drip.

"Morning." He put the groceries on the counter and set the duffel on the chaise. He opened it and pulled out a stack of my clothes. "Your books are in the car. Don't forget you have the levels exam today. Do you need to study for the written portion?"

I had forgotten. "No. What time is the test?"

"10 a.m. I'm your ride." It was just after seven.

"What level did you test as?" I had to ask.

"I never tested. Girls only."

"Except me." I sighed heavily and poured myself a cup of coffee.

Jamie pulled a small bottle of creamer out of one of the grocery bags. "Use this, please. It's one of Dr. Moler's simple changes. She actually wants you to switch from coffee to tea."

It was an organic whole-milk creamer. High fat, but it wasn't like I was drinking the whole thing at once. A dab in my cup and a drop of agave sweetener made the coffee just perfect. Jamie began pulling the rest of the groceries out. Some of them were things I ate regularly, and some I didn't care much for, like a flowered tea that looked like something old ladies would drink.

"She wants you to have a cup of this tea each time you're feeling anxious."

I must have made a face, because Jamie smiled his crooked smile and pulled out a fresh oversized bottle of my agave sweetener. "She said you can be as liberal as you want with the agave." He also gave me a pomegranate. "At least one a day. To help balance your system."

A small bottle of pills came out of a tiny prescription bag, and I was already shaking my head. "They are all natural. I even have a little journal here. Dr. Moler wants you to write anything you feel from these. Whether it's that they are working or they make you calmer or you feel nothing. Anything."

I sliced open the pomegranate, dug the insides out into a bowl, and ate them with a spoon. Drugs and I didn't mix. It wasn't for fear that I'd get addicted or that they really would work or it would prove I had some major issues. I couldn't take them because I just couldn't process them. Most made me throw up or just went straight through my system. Often I could taste the unnatural component.

"Do you promise you'll do your best on the test today?" Jamie asked.

"I told my mom I would."

"But will you do it? No throwing the test, getting answers wrong on purpose, not showing your power." He leaned against the counter in jeans and a sweater, looking confident and normal. I wished I was like him, but I would never measure up.

"You should test. You probably have more power than me."

He shook his head. "It was almost impossible to hold my animal form to find you. And it took forever to change. Gabe used your cell phone to figure out which tower the signal bounced off, and then we started from there. By the time we'd found your car, you were a day ahead of us. Then it took me almost three hours to change." Jamie shivered. "I've never hurt so much in my life. If I never change on a non-new-moon night again, that's fine with me."

"But you could. Most witches couldn't."

"It's never as complete a transition as yours was. I don't have enough earth flowing through me to cast off my humanity. Even as a bear, I'm still human—thoughts, actions, everything. When you go lynx, you go all the way. I was so afraid you'd never come back."

I sipped my coffee and ate my breakfast. "Why do you care? You barely know me."

"I know you better than you think." He went back to the chaise and pulled a box out of the bag and handed it to me.

"What is this?"

"Something I found at your place. I'm packing things up for you. Gabe asked me to. Said it would be too hard for you to go back."

The box was long and skinny and could only hold one thing, my Asian Ball Joint Doll. I set it on the counter and pried the top off and peered at the white pillow wrapping my most prized possession. Underneath would be the strong sculpted male body, unmarred, but the head had been shattered years ago. I'd tried to piece it together. Even tried to use my earth magic on it, but there wasn't enough organic material in it to mend it that way.

I rolled back the pillow and examined the body for damage. Still perfect. The string was a little loose. That was easily fixed. A plastic bag held the pieces of the shattered head. Off to the side, a small batch of clothes were bundled in an old candy box. This little destruction had almost broken me last time. Years had made me both stronger and weaker. I relied too much on Gabe and doubted everyone far too much.

"You look like a little boy being reunited with a lost puppy," Jamie remarked.

I scowled at him and put my dishes in the washer. "Run with me?" I needed to get the kinks out of my muscles before I got stuck inside a classroom for most of the day. They wanted to see what I could do? So be it. Be careful what you wish for could not have been more true.

"I'll do my best to keep up."

CHAPTER 12

Brock looked stunned to see me walking down the hall toward the temporary lockers outside the testing room. Everyone wanted me to take the damn test again. Show them what I could do. The Dominion planned to kill me anyway, right? So what the hell? I'd give them me in all my fucked-up glory.

Brock slid up beside me and watched me put away the heavy lunch bag Jamie had packed.

"You okay? The news said you'd gone missing."

"Not missing at all. Just taking some time away from the media." I'd come from a long run. Jamie had been a silent body-guard. He kept up well despite his size. Even maintained my pace for the seven-and-a-half miles I ran to get readjusted to my human form. My brain was still foggy, like it was pulling out of some weird dream. So I had run until my legs hurt and I knew it was me and not the lynx inside my head. I'd showered and changed into loose but clean running pants and a Bloody Bar T-shirt before grabbing a coat and heading to school.

Jamie set the timer on my watch to remind me to eat. He looked so happy when I took the bag, I could hardly tell him I had to leave it in a locker during the test. And whether the watch beeped or not, I would not be allowed to leave until everyone was finished with the written portion of the test.

"So you're really going to retake the test." Brock followed me to the classroom.

"I promised my mom I would. I keep my promises." I entered the room without him. Three guys sat grouped together in back, away from the army of girls that occupied most of the room. I recognized one guy from the track team. His platinum-blond hair and tan skin made him look like a beach bum. But I'd seen him run. Cheered our whole team on to the last semifinals. Would have watched them in the finals, but my mom had shown up asking if I was dating someone on the team. Blond Hair could run with me any time. He looked really hot in running shorts. I smiled in his direction and headed to the front to check in.

The classroom sat probably thirty girls, and every eye in the room gawked at me. No one ever retested. You took your results and left with whatever they were, low level or not. When I'd entered the magic studies program I was the only male studying and it was unprecedented. Retaking the test was even more so. It proved how much power my mother had and worried the hell out of me. It was like she wanted to paint another target on my back just because the first round of bullies hadn't killed me.

I walked up to Professor Kana Stout and presented myself. "Seiran Rou. Here for the earth magic proficiency test."

She nodded. "Have a seat, Seiran. We'll begin shortly."

I moved to an empty chair in the front of the room. The whispering began as soon as I sat down. I pulled out my reader and let the room fade away to the new romance I'd started during the drive. Jamie said that Gabe was having someone retrieve my car from wherever I'd left it in Iowa. I'd need it back eventually, but not today, so it didn't matter.

Brock sat down beside me. He gave me a warm smile and pulled out *Supernatural Vogue*, a magazine about lycans and vampires with money and fame. That he was taking the test surprised me a little. He seemed sort of a blend-in type, though I really hadn't known him all that long. He did hang with me on occasion, which probably earned him more than a handful of unusual stares.

Professor Stout rose from her chair and clapped her hands, just in time to interrupt the first love scene of my book. "Welcome to the proficiency test. For those of you who have not taken the test before, the procedure is simple. A forty-minute written exam will test your knowledge of basic Dominion Code. And individual testing in the applied series will set your element level. Do not be discouraged; most witches test at element level one. Those who have taken this test before"—her eyes fell to me— "will receive the forty-minute exam and a fifteen-minute essay before your applied testing."

I shrugged and pulled out two mechanical pencils. Jamie told me they used the first exam to see whether a witch would use his trained power properly or not. The essay I'd never done before, but I could write my way through just about anything. The applied section was always a breeze, even more so for me today if I didn't hold back. The number of applicants to the program was high this year. Though if you took into account the four other guys in the room and that the test was being held in the fall, not the spring as it usually was, there wasn't much normal going. Maybe the applied session would last long enough to let me skip tonight's party. Baby-mama picking didn't sound like a good way to spend a Friday night.

"Yes, Mr. Southerton?" Professor Stout asked.

"I'd like to take the essay as well." It was Brock. Had I ever asked his last name? I glanced his way, and he just smiled. "I would think if it's needed to gauge someone's skill for a retest, we should probably take it too."

"Fine. You may take the essay also. Anyone else?" she asked, then sighed in frustration a moment later. "Fine. Everyone may take the essay." Her eyes raked over me, but I hadn't raised my hand. "All materials away. I will pass out the tests and start the clock."

The door opened, and a group of girls walked in like they expected to be heralded as queens. I fought not to sink down in my seat. The queen bee of the five debutantes was a twenty-something earth witch who just happened to be the current earth Pillar, Rose Pewette. It was a terrible thing to name a girl after a flower, especially such a venomous girl. It was an insult to the flower and more than a little misleading.

She'd been the instigator of some of the most vicious attacks on me. Then there were her infamous hexes. The whole world seemed wrapped around her fingers. Why people like her could do no wrong made no sense. She violated more than two dozen Dominion Codes my first year of college. Yet I was the bad one simply for being a guy.

The girls moved across the room, flipping their collective blonde locks and swaying their hips like someone cared. I tried to keep my eyes glued to the board in front of me. No one could accuse me of cheating if I were in the front row and had no one sitting next to me. Unfortunately, Rose sat down in the empty seat to my right, and her posse fanned out around her.

"I'm here for a retest, Professor," she said, fake smile ever present. "Supporting my friends who are testing the first time."

The teacher seemed flustered for a few seconds, as if she were overwhelmed by Rose's presence. "Of course, Miss Pewette. Most of the class has elected to take the written essay as well. Would you like to join in?"

Rose's silence seemed to make everyone hold their breath until she tittered that terrible fake sound and said, "Sure. I can't wait to see how I score this time. As long as we all know I'm the most powerful earth witch in the room, no feelings will be hurt. Right?" I could almost feel her eyes on me. She couldn't hex me in front of the whole class, could she? Or worse yet, she probably would and no one would do anything about it. I sucked in a deep breath and gripped my pencils.

"Of course," the professor said and handed out the tests. I waited until time to start by staring straight ahead. The girls giggled and whispered things they had to know I could hear, the common theme being that I was a queer who murdered anyone I thought prettier than me. That certainly left Rose Pewette safe, though I didn't say so out loud, as it would likely get me hexed. I stared at the board and tried to pretend deafness had caught me at an early age. Maybe I should have been searching for invisibility spells all this time. Huh, that was a thought, wasn't it?

"Alright, everyone. Flip your paper and begin."

The standard portion of the test was easier than I remembered from four years ago. It was questions all straight from the Code, things from what level wards were legal to what punishment came with what hex. Rose should probably have the last part memorized.

The essay portion was different. There were three questions to choose from. I answered the one about why we needed the Dominion Code—explaining how low-level witches or ordinary humans could be hurt without it. I also spoke of the balance of nature and how without the Code, we'd likely have been a fiery ball of lifeless ash long ago. Maybe speaking of the Dominion's almighty benevolence would have gained me bonus points, but I only had fifteen minutes and couldn't find it in me to lie that deeply.

Once finished, I flipped the test over and raised my hand so the professor could collect it. No chance of shuffling papers or accidentally seeing someone else's answers if I didn't leave my seat or look anywhere but in front or at my paper. Too many years of having others examine my actions under a microscope had taught me better. I'd even worn my hair in a high ponytail so I couldn't be accused of spying through it. The professor collected my test, and I waited until everyone else was done. The talking began again.

"Now, class. We will have a half-hour lunch, and then you will all need to meet at the front of the school for the applied test. We'll be going to Minnesota Valley, and we'll all be divided up into two buses. Miss the bus, miss the rest of the test." We were dismissed with directions to where to meet up again.

My watch beeped just as I reached my borrowed locker. Thankfully, no one had broken into it or disturbed my lunch. Had Jamie known what time everyone would finish and we'd get a break? I shut off the alarm. Brock stood at my elbow.

"Lunch?" I asked. The bag was heavy, meaning there was probably enough for me and five Brocks.

"Sure."

We headed to the courtyard, near where our bus would be, and unpacked the lunch under a tree of falling maple leaves. I left the thermos filled with flowery tea in the bag, but pulled out several sandwiches, fruits, and a little pill holder with a note attached to the top. It said, "One with food, twice a day." The writing was Jamie's, and there was only one pill inside.

I sighed, took a sip of the water, and swallowed the pill before biting into one of the walnut bread, turkey, and provolone sandwiches. The pickles and mild hint of olive oil made me sigh with satisfied relief. Brock peeled the pickles off his and gave them to me, then devoured his sandwich in seconds.

"What's the pill for?" Brock asked quietly.

"Anxiety. I'm sort of OCD about some things. Get panic attacks sometimes."

Brock nodded like he understood. I wrote in my little notebook that the pill tasted woody but didn't seem to be making me throw it back up. I stuffed everything back inside the bag, and we headed toward the buses. Professor Stout ushered us all aboard. I sat right behind the driver with Brock. The professor took the seat across from us. Rose and her crew were the last to board, purposely shoving Brock as they passed. I stared out the window, pretending not to see them.

"Bitches," Brock mumbled.

"Amen," I heard from behind me and looked back at Blond Hair, who smiled back in a flirtatious sort of way. Debating the meaning of the runner's smile meant considering dating someone at school—something I didn't do. No one ever talked to me while on campus other than Brock, and he'd only begun to hang around me recently.

I took out my book reader and tried to ignore the feeling of growing apprehension in my stomach. It was a weird sense of foreboding that ran down my spine. Something bad was coming. A quick internal shake of the head, and then I focused on the book, reading about someone getting a good ass pounding by a hot guy with a sailor's mouth.

The girls sang songs from childhoods filled with witch camps during the hour-long drive. The guys all sat up front near Brock and me, reading magazines or talking about sports. When we arrived, we were greeted by three other professors. I'd had Brenda Wrig for more than one class. She was a level-three earth witch, and despite her advanced age and graying hair, nothing slipped by her.

"Seiran Rou. Back again. Level three wasn't good enough last time?" she asked me.

"Sorry, ma'am. Just fulfilling a promise to my mother."

She nodded her approval. "We'll start with you, then, since you can show the others how it's done."

We were led to the edge of a rushing stream, waterfall nearby, trees thick, and air whipping. The roll of earth calmed my nerves a little. I let it ease away the growing panic that had been building since I'd gotten on the bus. The professors would keep everyone safe. Even they wouldn't be able to ignore the blatant use of a hex if Rose decided I need to be made a fool of again. Plus, for once, I wasn't the only guy in the group.

Five elements, though since all witches had spirit, the fifth test would be unnecessary. Spirit determined the level of elemental power we had, but it was easier to just test the element.

Everyone would be tested for his or her inherited element—unless otherwise noted. I'd never tested for water, air, or fire. Both of my parents were earth, or so my mother said. We would watch the others test, keeping the higher-level witches free in case trouble started.

The four tests were held at four stations: a circular stone hearth with a fire raging in it for fire; an open spot to summon a cloud for air; a thin branch off of the stream, blocked by a minor dam, for water; and a dead tree stump for earth. Each test was small and focused on purpose. Safer that way. Easier to set a level.

Everyone broke into groups. Only three out of the bunch besides Rose and I were testing for earth; ten for fire, including Brock; seven for water, with Blond Hair leading that group; and the rest were air, the most common and often least powerful element.

Professor Wrig gestured to the stump. "Seiran, if you will demonstrate, please?"

Rose looked like she'd swallowed a lemon. "I can show them how it's done, Professor," she said.

"I'm sure you can, Miss Pewette. However, I already asked Mr. Rou."

I took a deep breath and stepped up to the stump, wondering if I was allowed to actually focus with the earth this time. "Can I kneel?" I asked Wrig quietly.

"Whatever you feel is necessary."

I knelt and waited for instructions.

Professor Wrig explained, "As Mr. Rou is showing you, he is putting himself in close contact with his element. He will be pulling power from the earth. Should he accidentally pull too much, he can give it back without causing damage to us or the surrounding area. He will take the time he needs to focus his power, and then he will place his hands to the stump. All witches with a measurable level will make something grow. A level one will produce moss or ivy. A level two will create flowers or even a small bud of a new tree. His level is set by what grows. Whenever you're ready, Seiran."

"Try not to kill any of us," Rose sneered from behind me.

I sighed, closed my eyes, and left all their scattered whispering behind. It didn't matter that Rose didn't shut up or that Blond Hair looked at me like he was imagining what sex with me would be like. The earth and I knew each other well. I let it flow through me, like I was nothing more than a pebble in a lake to be shaped and guided by it. Each breath brought renewed life. I set my hands to the stump, remembering the last time, when I'd made wildflowers burst forth from the dead tree. This time I didn't even look. The earth would grow what it wanted to with me as its conduit.

The power flowed through me in natural peaks and waves. The crowd gasped. The wood shifted and moved beneath my hands. I let the earth move as it wanted until the final wave subsided. Letting go, I opened my eyes and stared at a giant oak tree, leaves growing to a rich, vibrant green. No wildflowers this time. I smiled at the tree and patted its strong, new trunk, which split the old stump in half.

"Very good, Mr. Rou," Professor Wrig told me. She offered me a hand up. I stood, dusted off my pants, and went to the back of the line. "Next," she said.

And so began the testing. When Rose finally stepped up to the split stump and new tree, she scowled and refused to kneel. Her fancy high heels dug into the dirt as she put her hands to the tree. The confused tree lost all the healthy green leaves, then rebloomed new leaves, which promptly died and fell to the ground. She looked triumphant, and her friends clapped their hands like good little minions do. I felt sorry for the tree and hoped it wouldn't die from all the attention.

Before we moved on to the next test, I touched the tree and gave it a refocus of earth to settle it and directed its roots toward the stream so it would continue to grow. I'd have felt bad if Rose had really messed up the tree after I'd made it grow there. Sure, nature had a way and the tree might have split through the old stump eventually, but that would have been decades down the line. So it was sort of my fault if it didn't make it.

After their test each witch could go back to the bus and wait to leave, but usually they hung around to watch the rest of the tests. I wondered if it made those who'd never tested before nervous. The first time I'd taken the test I'd been more than a little on edge, but I'd also been trying to hide the level of my power. Rose Pewette had not been around the first time. Though maybe if she had she'd have treated me a little better. I debated returning to the bus for a minute but decided to join the group and at least watch Brock's test. Maybe he'd be less nervous with the support, or maybe he wasn't anxious at all. Either way it felt like something a friend should do. And we were friends weren't we?

Fire was a whole different sort of test. The professor in charge placed a log outside the hearth, then showed her group how to make the flame move to it and then back. None of the girls were able to copy the professor, though some made the fire spit or jump dangerously. When Brock stepped up, he copied the professor easily, even pushing the fire back until it went out, then relighting it with a flick of his hand. Everyone clapped quietly. He moved to stand beside me.

"Barely light a match?" I asked him.

He winked at me. "Remember that, eh?"

"Are you going to watch the other tests," I asked him.

"Sure. I'm curious. Are you?"

When we moved on to air, another of the professors stepped

up to show how it was done. She formed a nice fog around herself and let the wind pick up enough to blow it away. One of the girls and two of the guys I didn't know were able to pull a cloud down very close to the professor, but none of them were able to make it go away. She had to reset the test for each of them. Many got the air to move a tiny bit, and most seemed disappointed by that. Lower-level air witches. So far, none of Rose's friends had tested high in anything.

The final elemental test was as simple as the rest. Upstream, the heavy crash of water told us that, despite the size of the tiny stream, it came from something more powerful. The professor and leader of the water group stepped into the stream, feet bare despite the cold, and we all watched as the water poured over the banks feed from a larger body of water downstream and flowed fast enough over a small dam to look like a little waterfall. Then the professor eased her power out of the stream, slowing the flow of water to the smaller branch and pushing the rest back into the main flow of the river.

Blond Hair took his turn. He knelt beside the stream and put his hands into the water. A great gush of power washed through the stream. Everyone jumped back a few feet, but the water flowed nicely, making the mini waterfall and disappearing down-stream as he eased his power out. He looked a bit red faced and sheepish when he stepped away from the stream.

"Sorry. A little too much on the startup," he told the professor.

"Good recovery, though," she replied and gestured to the next student.

"That was Kelly," Brock told me. "He's part of our secret group too." Meaning the Ascendance, I thought. I pitied the guy for being named after a girl and wondered who his mom was. A high-level water witch, probably. Earth and water didn't mix. Sort of like two elite and very different aristocracies. I wondered what he turned into on the new moon.

The last girl to test was one of Rose's friends. She seemed an awkward girl, not usually the cliché type. Her hair was not as perfect, body a little chubby. Rose's hissed whisper of "You better make us look good, Bernie" gave me a bad feeling.

Bernie stepped into the water, fear on her face. I felt the power before it hit the stream and knew something was about to go wrong.

With a rumble and a roar, water poured away from the main channel of the river and came rushing toward us. It hit the trees, which trembled and shook at its force, many cracking under the pressure. There was screaming. The water professor was trying to redirect the flood, talking calmly to Bernie to help her focus the flow. The other professors ushered everyone away from the rising water. It reached my ankles before I knew that there was no way they were going to be able to stop the flood, and we'd never make it to the buses in time. How many would it kill?

Brock grabbed my arm and told me to go. Everyone else moved, trying to outrun the water. Kelly had thrown himself into the stream, probably trying to help them keep the water back, but having broken free, it was a force to be reckoned with. It needed somewhere to go, something to stop its path of destruction. Kelly could kill himself trying, but the most powerful water witch couldn't stop that flood without help.

The hard, dry stretch of the ground told me it hadn't rained here in weeks. The forest was thirsty, and the trees needed the nourishment. But this flood was just too much for it to take at once, not without encouragement. I knelt beside Kelly, hands to the earth, searching for those scattered seeds that would have found purchase in the warm thaw of the spring that was still months away. If this didn't work, we'd both die. In fact, a lot of us would die, because that wall of water was like something out of a disaster movie. My power reached all those scattered pinecones, seeds, and sleeping plants, and I willed them to drink as much as they could hold—pressing life energy into those seeds, forcing the accelerated growth of trees, whose flourishing roots strained to suck up the coming water. Kelly must have felt the pull of my power, because he directed the water in a further spread, out into the forest, soaking everyone around us but scattering it to be taken by the earth in a wide range.

The ground erupted with hundreds of madly growing pine trees, all absorbing the water even as it flowed toward us. The earth fueled the trees. I willed them to take as much as they could and prayed that, when the water hit, it wouldn't hurt quite so much. Several thick, heavy roots rose from the ground and wrapped around Kelly and me.

Brock and the other two guys lunged forward, clinging to Kelly and me as the water hit with a hearty slap. It pounded into our small group for several seconds, turning the ground at our feet into mud and threatening to wash us away. Still I fought to hold on to the pulsing energy of the earth and the tremendous waves that lapped around our legs. Only the roots wrapped around our bodies kept us from being rushed downstream.

The flow of the earth through me fed the trees as they grew into towering pines. When it ended, we knelt in less than a half foot of quickly receding water, all shivering, but safe. A brand-new forest had sprung from our misadventure, looming over us like the redwoods of California. The forest felt happy, alive, and awake, though the explosion of growth had been exhausting to me at least. Not all the new trees would survive, but the rich dirt beneath us welcomed the roots that continued to bury themselves deeper readying for the cold of winter.

The roots that held us curled back into the ground, disappearing as if they'd never broken the surface. The silence echoed heavily around us until the chirping of birds and the roar of the falls in the distance were all we could hear. Kelly and I clung together, both shaking with the amount of power that had poured through us. It was nonsexual, but that didn't stop the girls from commenting.

"Get a room, fags."

Professors Wrig and Stout brought towels and emergency blankets. I helped Kelly up. We were covered in mud. My hands were caked in the stuff and the ground was slick and sloppy beneath us. We took our towels and made our way back to the bus while continuing to hold each other up. I really could have used a nap.

Everyone all piled back onto the buses, subdued and tired. No one had been seriously hurt—which shocked me. There were a few grumbles about sprained ankles and nasty retorts about ruined clothes, but that seemed to be the worst of it.

Kelly and I sat together, shivering from the water that had drenched our clothes. Brock jammed himself in beside us, and suddenly warmth began to radiate our little area.

"In the middle," Kelly said and let Brock slide over him to sit between us. Then the heat hit me at full force, and I curled around Brock. Kelly mirrored me on the other side. Our clothes began to dry, but I knew we both looked a mess. Rose made some comment about the three little pigs sitting in the front seat. I briefly wished she'd been swept away.

I pulled my bag from beneath the seat and poured myself some of that flowered tea. The shaking in my hands subsided after the first cup, and I offered some to Kelly, who accepted quietly, and Brock who declined with a "maybe later."

The bus headed back to campus, where our scores would be announced. I hoped it would be fast because I needed a warm shower something fierce. The hour drive passed, and I must have dozed. When we pulled into the lot, I noticed Jamie's car immediately. Did he know something had happened? The lot was full of parents rushing to the bus for their daughters. Someone must have reported the incident. Jamie leaned up against the wall outside the main entrance until I got off the bus with Kelly and Brock in tow. He pushed away from the wall and walked toward me, looking a lot like all those overprotective parents.

"I'm okay," I said immediately, but he wrapped his arms

around me in a hug that felt hard enough to bust ribs. "Air!" I cried. He let me go, looking a little teary. "I'm okay. Really. It was just a little water."

Brock disappeared into the group. I saw Kelly get a tight hug from a small woman with his gray eyes and long dark hair. His mom, maybe?

"I think I made a new friend," I told Jamie as he led me into the building, back to the lecture room where we'd taken the written test. We would normally receive our results right away, as long as the incident hadn't delayed anything. All the desks had been converted to rows of seats.

Shit. My mom waited inside the classroom.

Jamie gripped my hand and pulled me to a seat in the front.

My mother moved across the room and sat down on the other side of me. "Hello, James," she said absently.

I looked at Jamie. Did they know each other? "Tanaka" was all he said, sounding neutral as hell.

"I'm surprised you didn't take the test." Her voice was cold. "Your father would have loved that."

"He's dead. He doesn't get to love anything anymore. You made sure of that." Jamie sat stiffly.

"If you two are going to fight, how about letting Seiran sit with us?" Brock said over my shoulder. He and the other guys sat together in the row behind us. They moved enough to open a seat in the middle for me. I glanced at Jamie, who shrugged and nodded, before I practically leapt over the chair to sit with them. I'd never had student friends before. Not even comrades-in-arms, like it seemed that we had become.

"Southerton, your mother should be ashamed of you," my mom said. "Mouthing off to elders."

"Not mouthing, ma'am. Just asking for your son's company, since he helped save our lives today. Without him and Kelly, we'd all probably be dead." Brock smiled at her like butter wouldn't melt in his mouth.

My heart still pounded. I dug into my bag for more of that damned tea but found that we'd drunk it all on the bus. Jamie leaned over his bag and pulled out a fresh thermos filled with tea and a small bottle of agave. I traded him the empty thermos for the full one. I'd never been so thankful for that awful flower brew. Unlike Brock's warmth, which had started from the outside, the tea's heat pooled up from the inside. I poured another cup for Kelly. He muttered a thank-you as the professor stepped up to the front of the room.

"Let's begin, shall we?" She started at the bottom and worked her way up. Most of the class learned that they were level-one witches.

The two guy air witches were ranked level three. Impressive. The crowd made a lot of noise, since all the girls so far had been ranked level two or lower.

"Bernice Mason is ranked level four in the element of water." The girl who'd almost killed us. Great. The professor paused before saying, "Brock Southerton is ranked level four in the element of fire." Noise grew as she continued to list the results. "Kelly Harding is ranked level five in the element of water." The grumbling of the crowd grew so loud the professor had to shush the room. "Rose Pewette and Seiran Rou are both ranked level five in the element of earth."

The room erupted in angry shouts of women screeching about how their daughters should have been ranked higher, how no male should have been rated so high. My mother looked triumphantly back at me from her seat ahead of us. I tried to avoid her gaze, sinking low in my seat. Jamie smiled encouragingly but couldn't hide his worry.

Professor Stout shushed the room again. "Today we witnessed an amazing feat. Two students came together to save the class from terrible danger. Though the Dominion recognizes that these two students are both male, they will be offered positions within the Dominion Council upon graduation."

Kelly and I stared at each other. I wondered if I looked as horrified as he did.

"Without the quick thinking of Seiran Rou and Kelly Harding, many of you would be mourning your children today. I am pleased to welcome all five male students to the Magic Studies program here at the University of Minnesota. Seiran will be graduating soon, but he seems to have paved the way for other very honest young men to become helpful witches in society."

I'd paved the way? I gulped down more of the tea and hoped we got out of this place soon. The professor stepped away from the front of the room, grabbed a stack of papers, and began calling our names to hand back our graded tests. The noise of the room got so loud it was closing in on me. Brock handed me my test. I thanked him and headed for the door, needing to be free from the terrible human cage.

Jamie followed me outside, waiting until I sank to my knees in the grass and felt the earth flowing in that calm rhythm again before speaking. "How'd you do on the test?" He took the paper from me and sat down beside me. "Nice. Only one wrong on the question portion. You only get jail time for a level three or above hex. Death's reserved for curses."

"Maybe it was wishful thinking," I muttered.

"They gave you a full twenty-five points for the essay. Even wrote that you have an eloquent way of writing." Jamie pulled another sandwich out of his bag. "Eat, please."

"I'm not hungry."

"After all the energy you used up today saving the masses from a flood? Eat."

The sandwich actually tasted pretty good. Roasted eggplant with smoked red peppers and spicy mustard. "You're raiding all my recipes, aren't you?"

"Yep. I like how you mark things with stars on the corners, five being the best. I'm not that great of a cook, but I can make a

144

sandwich." He got out a brush. "Your hair is a mess. Can I comb it?"

I shrugged, finishing up the sandwich he'd given me. My mom strolled up just as I was swallowing the last piece, which went down like stone.

"Calm," Jamie said.

"Don't forget the party tonight, Seiran. You should cut your hair." She frowned at Jamie, who was brushing my hair like it was really important to him. "Dress nice tonight. You have a suit, right? You're level five; that means all the girls will want you."

"For a sperm donor?"

"You could marry one of the girls. Have a normal life."

"No, Mom. I never had a chance for a normal life, did I?" How long had she known I was a level five? Had all my years of stealth been worthless? I sighed. She really would kill me as soon as my baby was born. I wondered if I could convince Gabe to take me to the Amazon or something. There was a lot of earth there. We could survive a while on the land. Although I was pretty sure they had spiders as big as dogs, and unless I was a lynx, I wouldn't go near a spider. That might be a deal breaker for me.

"You will come to the party."

"I said I would, so I will. Just like I promised to take the test. I keep my word." I couldn't look at her anymore. Even connected to the ground as I was, the tremors began in my hands. Jamie put his arm around my waist from behind. My mother shook her head and walked away. "She probably thinks I'm sleeping with you," I told Jamie.

"She can believe whatever she wants."

Brock and Kelly approached. Jamie stopped brushing my hair. It was just after three in the afternoon. "Want to come over for an early dinner?" I asked. "I'm a pretty good cook."

"Sure," Kelly said.

"The girls are talking about some sort of party tonight. Saying it's to choose your wife." Brock looked angry.

"Nope. No wife for me. My mom is demanding an heir, so she is going to pick a baby momma. I'm not even sure why I have to do this party." I got up and held a hand out to Jamie to help him up.

"Do you have to sleep with her until she gets pregnant?" Kelly asked, his face twisted with distaste.

"No," Jamie answered for me. "If Tanaka wants a baby from Seiran, she'll have to pick a woman willing to use a turkey baster."

We all laughed.

CHAPTER 13

"Why are there three attractive young men asleep on my couch? Not that I'm protesting," Gabe said from somewhere far away. I stretched and Kelly's warmth moved next to me. We'd all gone to Gabe's place downstairs, where I'd showered, then made a light early dinner for them—not being hungry myself—and we promptly fell asleep.

Jamie's voice was hushed as he talked about the day's adventure and how I scored on the levels test. "Sei and Kelly are both level five. Brock is four."

"Doesn't surprise me about Sei." He moved across the room.

I looked at him through sleepy eyes. "Will you go to the party with me?"

"Of course. I figured if you didn't ask, I would send Jamie so you didn't feel I was pushing you." He was adjusting a long-sleeve button-down. Gucci, I was sure. "It's getting late. Did your friends drive themselves, or do they need a ride home?"

Jamie grabbed the keys off the hook beside the door. "I'll drive them back to their cars." I shook Brock and Kelly awake. They moved sleepily to the door, thanking me for the food and promising to call this weekend. Brock reminded me of the secret party tomorrow night. Kelly laughed at that, but both left with Jamie.

Gabe sat down next to me, grabbed a fistful of my hair, and kissed me viciously. The pain of his grip was a wonderful contrast to the sweetness of his lips and skilled tongue. He seemed to want to devour me for several minutes, and I was okay with that. When he finally pulled away, he rested his head against mine. "You are so beautiful."

I started to say, "Fucked up," but he stopped me with a finger to my lips.

"Growing up can work out some of those gangly limbs."

"What's that mean?"

"You're becoming the man I knew you would be. Smart—" He kissed my forehead. "—beautiful—" Another kiss, this time to my cheek. "—caring—" Finally his lips found mine, and then he whispered, "My focus."

I didn't get that either, but he looked so serious, I wanted to jump him and get him to fuck my brains out.

He laughed. "Everything you feel is on your face. You know that, right? I don't think we have time for sex before the party. You were supposed to be there at seven. It's almost eight."

"How about a quickie? I never did get to return the favor the other night."

He raised a golden brow. "What favor was that?" I pushed him back against the sofa, unbuttoned his pants, and pressed my face into the soft musky scent of his balls. He groaned. "That favor. Okay."

Watching him fill and grow as his pulse jumped in my hand was as beautiful as watching a flower bloom on a high-speed camera. He shimmied his pants down to his ankles, allowing his knees to spread, giving me better access. I licked around his thick, heavy balls, teasing and nipping at the sensitive flesh of his inner thigh.

"You're killing me, Sei."

"Hmm?" I asked, flicking my tongue up his length to dip into his slit, which made him arch his back.

Kissing lightly down the side, I laid butterfly kisses all over him, more to tease him than anything else. He shivered. "What could you mean?" I asked before I sucked gently on his foreskin, knowing how sensitive the head would be.

He writhed and opened farther for me, and I dipped down low so I could taste his sweet ass while I stroked his cock slower than I knew he'd like me to. Usually he was the one teasing me. It was nice to be in charge for once and watch him come apart from my touch.

"Shit, Sei. Suck me."

I smiled at him but continued to lick at his hole, diving inside with my tongue. I wet two fingers and replaced my tongue with them, pressing deep enough to almost hit his prostate. Then I swallowed him down until I felt him at the back of my throat, humming around him and finding that spongy, wanting spot inside all at once. He writhed against me, forcing himself farther down my throat. I fisted part of him to ease up what I had to swallow and pounded my fingers hard into him, the way I knew he liked it. Gabe liked his sex a little rough. Why he still wanted me so much when I was not exactly the kind of guy who could wrestle him down and fuck him blind, I didn't know. But I'd learned how to make him tremble. I squeezed his balls a little harder than I would have liked, scraping the head of his cock with my teeth and teasing his slit with my tongue.

He came, shooting down my throat and arching against me. I had to fight to keep from being choked in his excitement. He thrust himself into my mouth several more times, until his release was spent, and I popped off him to let the overly sensitive tip free from the sweet torture.

I licked him clean and gave him more baby kisses down the side of his softening flesh. He pulled me up into his lap, and in a heated kiss, we shared the taste. He was the only guy I was with that ever did that. Most would have pushed me away or told me to clean up before kissing. Come was kind of gross for most people. I didn't mind it, and obviously neither did Gabe.

We stayed like that for a while—kissing like it was all we had left to do in the world—long enough that I felt his erection coming back.

"How much QuickLife have you had today?" I asked, reaching down to deliver a long pull to help along his happy.

"I don't need as much down here. My grave soil is here. It's almost like being human. Plus there's this really hot guy who really makes me hard with just a look."

"Yeah? Do I know him?" I teased.

He grinned.

I just looked at him, trying to read his expression. He seemed to be doing the same thing to me. "Sometimes you seem to know what I'm thinking. What am I thinking now?"

"That's not hard. You want me to fuck you. But you always want that."

"Is that a bad thing?"

"Not at all. I enjoy fucking you. But what I really enjoy is when you let me make love to you." He pressed me into the sofa and slid his hand under my shirt to play with the nipple rings I'd put back in after he'd left them beside the bed this morning. "I wish we had more time to play tonight."

I groaned, and not in a good way. "Can't we just skip the party? It's not like she really needs me there anyway."

"And lose my chance to dance with you? You did ask me to go, after all." His green eyes practically glowed with happiness.

"I don't get you. You know that, right?"

Gabe smiled, then kissed from my chin down to my collarbone. "Oh, you get me. You just don't get you. But you're getting there. You made friends. I'm so proud of you."

"It's not my fault no one has ever liked me before."

"I hope Brock and Kelly are worthy of your hard-won friendship."

"Hard-won?"

He let me go, rose from the couch, and adjusted his clothes. He stepped over to the computer, hit a few keys, and a picture popped up. It was a family: man, woman, and child. Gabe gestured to the chair. "Sit here for a bit while I clean up and get changed. I'll find something nice for you to wear tonight that won't upset your mother too much."

I began to protest, but he stopped me with a kiss. "Look at the picture, and when I come back, tell me what you see."

Sighing, I watched him leave the room, then stared at the picture on the screen. The kid had brown eyes, blond hair. Fairly normal. He looked a lot like the woman. Big kind-of-crooked smile on the kid's face.

I frowned. Was this Jamie?

The closer I looked, the more I knew it had to be him. He was probably five or six. He had told me his mom and dad hadn't loved each other. They didn't look like they had even *liked* each other much. Neither smiled. Both looked tired, especially the man, who had shadows under his bright blue eyes. He was a beautiful man. Jamie should be happy to be handsome in a more rugged way. I knew from experience that being pretty and male was not an easy thing.

The man in the picture would have known my pain. His hair was paler than mine, more of a rich brandy, his eyes sapphire blue.

Just like mine.

I sucked in a deep breath, felt pain rise in my chest. It couldn't be. I looked at Jamie's young face and saw the traces of resemblance between the two. A panic attack began wriggling its way up my spine like the dark monster it was. I made my way to the kitchen gripping my chest and the counter all at once. I breathed in and out, trying to steady myself. It couldn't be, could it?

A thermos of tea sat on the counter with a note from Jamie to keep drinking it. I went through the whole thing before I started to calm.

Gabe exited the bedroom, looking like the handsome millionaire he was.

"He's my dad—the guy in the picture—right?" I asked Gabe, pulling open my notebook to write how the tea had helped calm me. I could breathe again, but my heart still thudded in my chest like it had forgotten how to work. Maybe it was because my head was so messed up.

"Was, yes. He's gone now."

"Jamie stalks me, tries to take care of me, because my dad died right before I was born?"

"Yes and no. I suspect since you've never had a real family, you don't know how family should act." Gabe moved to stand beside me in the kitchen and stared down at the journal, which was mostly empty. "Do you need me to say it?"

"I think so. But don't be surprised if I fall apart."

He wrapped his arms around me. His breath was warm on my neck. "You won't fall apart. You're the strongest person I know. Didn't you help stop a flood today? Become the first male in history to be declared a level-five earth witch?" He paused, then said, "Jamie is your brother."

"He's really my brother?"

"Yes. How do you feel about that?"

"Weird, considering how many times I've come on to him. Why you didn't tell me?"

"How would you have reacted if I'd told you as soon as I hired him on at the bar?" His look told me he knew exactly how I would have reacted. "You ran into him at school right before you were attacked and nearly raped. Remember that time I took you to the hospital? If I'd tried to introduce you or even if he'd come your way himself, what would you have done?"

"I would have quit fearing he was a spy sent by my mother."

Probably avoided Gabe. Where would I be then? No job, no home, no Gabe.

"Exactly. I warned Jamie to keep quiet, but that wasn't going to keep him away."

I sighed and glared at the picture from across the room, feeling a whole crapload of mixed-up emotions. I had a brother. Who would have thought? And my mom must have known since she'd recognized him at school today. Did he have any idea how much I could have used a brother growing up? But Gabe was right. I would have pushed Jamie away to try to protect myself.

Gabe patted my head and let me go. "That's why I told you to keep your hands off. Not because he and I have anything together. Understand?"

All I could do was nod. He led me to the bedroom and pointed out the attire he'd picked out for the evening. Thankfully it wasn't a suit like his. Nice pants, a soft button-down in a blue that matched my eyes, and shiny black shoes. All knockoffs, since I never liked him spoiling me with expensive things.

"Why'd he take so long to come around?" I asked.

"I suspect you know the reason to that."

Yeah. Mostly because of my mom. I sighed. Could I ever catch a break? "I probably look like an idiot to him. Dumb baby brother he has to take care of."

"Not how he sees you at all."

"Hmm," I answered absently as the elevator door opened and the sound of Jamie returning filled the apartment. Gabe shut the bedroom door to let me dress. Would he tell Jamie that he'd told me? Was it a secret? I dressed quickly and returned to the living area.

I found Jamie in the kitchen, where he checked the thermos of tea and put a kettle on to refill it. He pulled a bottle out of a drawer and picked up a small bowl of fruit before handing them to me. "Pill, then eat, please."

I did my best not to choke on the pill and devoured the fruit. I felt his eyes on me and suddenly realized I had to be lacking. I couldn't be the brother he wanted. Whatever it was that he saw when he looked at me couldn't be *me*. He obviously had some idealistic image of what a little brother should be or how an older brother should take care of his sibling. Life didn't work that way. People just weren't nice to me. Except, he was.

He washed both thermoses and refilled them with tea. "You should take the tea with you. It seems to calm your nerves," Jamie told me.

"What's in that stuff, anyway?"

"Lilac, maple bark, hyacinth. All natural stuff. I believe the idea is to give you the earth from inside out, since you're an earth witch. That's why Dr. Moler wants you to go to all organic foods." He pulled out my walnut bread—there wasn't much left— and bagged up a tomato cheese sandwich and put it with the fresh thermos of tea. "Don't eat that crap at the party. There's no telling what might be in it." He flipped through my notebook of recipes. "Is the walnut bread in here?"

"Middle," I said. Maybe, since tomorrow was Saturday, I could cook. Something to look forward to, as Gabe always said. "There's a banana rosemary bread that is really tasty, even though it sounds funny." Jamie made a face but marked the page with a green sticky note.

A party tonight and tomorrow night. Any other time, I'd be prowling for dates. I stared at Gabe, who looked so beautiful in his Armani suit over the Gucci shirt, jacket flung over the back of the couch and sleeves rolled up, and wondered why I ever looked elsewhere for company. His dark blond hair had a carefree style, like so many models did nowadays. Yet I knew if I touched it, his hair would feel soft and product free. On his face, he'd even left just a touch of the stubble I loved so much when he kissed me. He was solid. Always there when I needed him. Had been for years. Of course, deep in my gut, I feared he'd leave me, but even Matthew hadn't stayed so long.

Jamie nudged me. "Huh?" I asked.

"You were practically drooling. The two of you should get going. I'm going back to your place to pick up some more of your stuff. Anything you need?"

"My clothes. All of them. And all the books."

"Books are already here. I put them in the library. You might want to tackle that tomorrow. I'm not sure how you had them arranged. I'll get your clothes. Need any dishes or knives you don't have here?"

I shook my head. "There is a bottle of white wine in the fridge. It's a limited holiday wine."

"I'll bring that too."

Should I hug him or something? Say that I knew? Tell him to take care, since we were going out? Gabe pulled me toward the door, scooping up his jacket on the way. "Night, Jamie," he said.

"Night," my brother replied as the door shut behind us.

Gabe was pretty good at reading me, so when we got in the car he took my hand and said, "What's wrong? Is it that you know Jamie is your brother now?"

"No." And it wasn't. It was a combination of everything. I was really messed in the head, wasn't I? "I never thought I'd be one of those dads that just abandon their kid." Never thought I'd ever be a dad at all.

"So don't be."

"Right, 'cause my mom didn't blackmail me with the threat of imprisonment if I didn't give her an heir." I tugged my hand out of his as he steered us toward my mom's house.

"I mean, don't abandon the baby. Just because your mom says she'll raise it doesn't mean she should. You don't have to give up any rights to this baby. You can be there for him or her as much as you want. I think you'd make a great dad." He paused. "A little neurotic, but I think that's important for new parents anyway."

I glared at Gabe. "Neurotic?"

"OCD?"

Yeah, I guessed I was OCD. If it meant cleaning and turning things off way more than most people. "And if the baby spits up all over the kitchen, I'll freak."

"You'll clean it up like you always do. You can also teach the baby to read and cook and run."

"Yeah, babies do all that?" I knew what he meant but just wanted to be contrary.

"Eventually. Though they will always be your baby no matter how old they get." He sighed and took my hand back. "Choose a mother you can live with. Not in the sense of actually cohabitating with her, but someone you feel you can negotiate with. Someone who will allow you to have a say."

"Unlike my mother." I wondered if my dad would have had any control over how I was raised if he were still alive.

"Tanaka is used to being in charge. Jamie said she had a difficult time with your birth and losing your dad in the middle of it just made her shut down."

"So he's saying she was nice before she had me?"

Gabe grinned and shook his head. "I don't think he'd go that far. And it wasn't about you. It was about your dad."

"So she hates me 'cause of who my dad is?" But I knew nothing of my dad. Maybe someday I'd get up enough courage to ask Jamie about him. He'd been young, too, when our dad died, but he had to know more than I did.

"I don't think she hates you. She doesn't quite know how to love you, but she doesn't hate you—despite all the horrible parenting mistakes she made."

I snorted at him. Was he kidding? I was lucky to have survived my childhood. "I'm surprised she didn't drown me in the tub when I was a kid."

He sighed. "My point is that you need to decide what you want to do. Be the dad you always wanted, or the one you had. Even if the girl you pick is a crappy mom, you still get to decide who you are and how you'll treat your kid."

I growled at him and stared out the window for a few minutes before finally saying, "Why do you gotta be so smart?"

"You would have come to the conclusion on your own eventually. Sometimes I think it's just emotionally easier if I tell you first, like you don't believe yourself for some reason. But we're working on that. And I like who you're becoming."

"I'm not changing to suit you," I grumbled, though I didn't really know why I was still arguing with him. He had plenty of valid points.

"And I'm not expecting you to. But don't think I haven't noticed that you're not out every night with a new guy anymore or that you don't often look beyond me when you need a quick fuck. Even when I'd rather have more."

"Just 'cause you're the cleanest guy I know...." I glared at him. "Don't get cocky."

"Never," he promised.

"Why do you stay when I'm such a jerk?"

"Because you're not a jerk. You're a little neurotic."

"OCD," I corrected.

"Neurotic," Gabe supplied, "but not a jerk. Now put on your game face, we've just entered the outer rung of hell." Gabe parked us on the street across from my mom's house.

The designer cars lining the road and hordes of finely dressed people headed toward the house proved Gabe right. We'd just arrived in hell.

CHAPTER 14

People lingered around my mother's mansion like she was the queen of England or something. Everyone stared when Gabe and I stepped out of his sports car. First impressions were everything, he told me. I reminded him that there probably wouldn't be a person at this party who hadn't met me before. But none of that mattered. He wanted to show us off as confident, happy, and unflappable. I wanted to get in and out as quickly as possible.

Seeing Rose Pewette and a flock of admirers in my mother's foyer made me mad enough to spit nails. Turkey baster or not, Rose was *not* going to be the mother of my child. She was dressed as a glam-queen, from the glittery barrettes that almost looked like a tiara to the sparkling Louboutin shoes. Her falseness made me want to throw a table at her. Or maybe a hex. How would she like that, eh? I'd have to learn a few first. My memory of them was kind of sketchy.

The whole room froze when I entered—every eye turning to stare at me. Gabe stepped up to my side and took my hand in his. He looked rich, powerful, and dangerous. But then, he'd done this sort of thing before, I was sure.

My mother rushed down the stairs and fussed with my shirt and hair. "Why didn't you cut it?"

"Because I like it long," Gabe answered curtly so I didn't have to.

She glared at him, then looked back to me. "You need to make your rounds, Seiran. You know how to greet everyone."

I gripped her arm and pulled her toward the empty study. Gabe did not follow us inside. Instead he shut the door behind us, waiting outside like a guard.

"You will not give Rose my baby."

"She's the Pillar of earth. You could hope for no better match. Two level-five earth witches," my mother argued.

"No! If you plan to do that, then tell me now. I will set *myself* on fire and save the rest of you the trouble."

"Don't be so dramatic."

"Were you ever going to tell me I have a brother? What else are you hiding from me other than wanting Rose to be my baby momma so you can kill me when the baby's born? Is Daddy still alive too?"

"James should not be telling you things."

"Why?" Maybe I should ask Jamie what he knew about my mom.

"His father was disreputable."

"But he was my father too. Is that why you hate me so much? 'Cause he was disreputable?" Her lips thinned and I could almost hear her grinding her teeth. I sighed. "I don't want to fight with you. You want an heir, fine. But not Rose, nor any of Rose's girl posse. They will torture that child. She put more than a dozen hexes on me my first year at college. The only thing Rose deserves is three to five in a women's penitentiary."

"You never told me you knew who did those things!"

How did my mom know about the hexes? She'd never been there. I'd never called her after an attack. Even after filing many police reports, I'd never heard a word from her. Not that

I'd ever felt the sudden urge to spill all my worldly troubles to her.

"She admitted it," I said. "She had two of her ex-boyfriends try to rape me. One of them beat me bad enough to send me to the ER." No need to mention that I'd broken his leg so badly that he never played football again. "Griped *loudly* when I moved off campus and wouldn't tell her where. No babies for Rose Pewette." Ryan Federoff had been dating Rose at the time he'd attacked me. I never saw him again after the attack. But I'd heard he dropped out when he lost his football scholarship. Funny how he never pressed charges against me for breaking his leg. Better to just suck it up, I guess, than revealing he'd been beaten up by a small queer boy-witch he'd tried to rape. I heard he'd been telling others he tripped and fell down the stairs. Which was probably better for me because the Dominion would have come in and ripped me apart for using my magic that way.

"Fine." She crossed her arms over her chest, like she was waiting for me to demand more, but I didn't need anything else. "Shall we make a list of who not to pick?"

"How about you let me pick?" I suggested.

"Fine. But you have only until the end of the month to decide before I choose for you."

I blinked back my shock. Was she really giving me control? "Really?"

She shrugged. "You're not a child anymore, Seiran. I want you to make your own decisions. Just remember you have to live with them when they turn bad as well."

Okay, on that happy note... I headed out the door. Thankfully, I hadn't started shaking. Maybe the tea really was doing more than making me have to piss every two hours.

Gabe raised a brow in my direction, but I shook my head, took his hand—squeezing it hard—and let him lead me in the direction of the patio. We didn't need words to express anything.

He probably saw my inner panic. And just like he always did, he knew I needed a few minutes away from everyone else.

The evening was chilly enough to make me wish I'd brought a coat. Gabe pulled me against him, and we danced slowly to the soft jazz flowing from the live band stationed on the second floor. He was warm, arms strong and solid. I wondered if he'd ever had kids. Two thousand years was a long time without a single one. But he'd never offered the information, and I gave those who did not push me for info the same respect in return.

The ancient oak trees surrounding the patio were a relaxing memory. There was still a carving in the trunk of the middle one with my name. And I was pretty sure the roots had swallowed a couple of the army figures I played with as a kid. I loved those trees. I could hide in their branches as a kid, and in their shadows now as an adult.

"I texted Jamie and asked him to bring you the Burberry I bought you. He's on his way." I nodded against Gabe's shoulder. He felt a bit like a wall himself, in tune with the earth and keeping all the madness at bay. Girls drifted around us on the patio dance floor. Some seemed to pause, maybe wondering if they could cut in, but none tried. I would have refused them all anyway. I needed to be shielded from the world sometimes.

Gabe's phone rang loudly. He groaned, but ignored it. When it stopped and started again, he pulled it out of his pocket. "If it's Jamie, I'm going to kill him."

Something changed in his face as he peered at the caller ID. He gave me a quick peck on the cheek. "Gotta take this. Sorry." He flipped open the phone and walked to the quiet end of the patio.

"Seiran?" a female voice asked, making me dread this party even more. At least she pronounced my name right. I turned to face a pretty young woman with fiery red hair cut pixie short around her face and large brown eyes that reminded me of Jamie. Freckles decorated the bridge of her nose. A waif of a girl, but she actually had two inches in height on me. She held out her hand. "Hanna Browan."

"Jamie's sister?" She looked a little like the woman in the picture, but definitely not old enough to be his mom.

"Yes. He and I have the same mother, different fathers."

"So you and I aren't related." One surprise sibling in a lifetime was enough.

"No." She looked me over. "He must be taking good care of you. You look better than you did the last time I saw you. He practically raised me, so it's not like he hasn't done it before."

"We met before?"

"You were in some of my classes a couple years ago. I'm a level-four earth witch. I work in the judicial branch of the Dominion. First time I saw you, I think you were eighteen. You'd already been at school a semester. You looked so haunted. The college girls were mean—even to other girls. I can't imagine how they would treat the only boy." She gave me a strained smile. "But we're practically family now."

I shook my head. "I don't do well with family. I'm sorry; I gotta go." I turned away to find Gabe, but she grabbed my hand. He was still on the phone and seemed to be arguing with someone.

"We can help each other, Seiran."

"I'm sure you're a nice girl, but my mom is a real bitch. We're a crazy lot. She sees you talking to me, she'll think you want to have my baby."

"I do."

"What?"

She gestured to a very glamorous, sort of pinup-looking girl who lingered on the edge of the patio by the door to the house. "My partner and I would love a child. I'm a high-level witch, so the Dominion is pushing me to have a baby." She frowned. "Some of their antiquated ways really need to be changed, but anyway, I'd rather it be with you than some stranger. If it's a boy—" She smiled briefly. "—I hope you'll still let us get to know him. And if it's a girl, I hope you will still love her. I do strongly believe that children have a lot to learn from both parents, no matter the sex of the baby or the parents."

It sounded rehearsed, and I stared at her. "Are you for real?"

"Don't get me wrong. This baby thing scares the crap out of me. But Allie has read all the baby books. She's excited. We plan to do this right. Jamie has told me all the horror stories about your mother. She scares me, but I know the law inside and out. Even a Pillar wouldn't get away with hurting our baby."

"You're a lawyer?"

"A judge. Fifth division." Which meant she dealt with everything from family law to murder.

"I'd still get to see the baby? Without my mom there? Even if it's a girl?" Would a kid be able to tell right away how messed up I was? Would I slap him or yell at him if he made a mess? The thought brought the tremor back to my hands.

"Yes."

"Is this why Jamie has been getting so close to me?" So he could use me to get his sister a baby?

"I don't think Jamie knows anything about my baby plans. I haven't said anything to him. He's been obsessed with you for years. Kept bringing me copies of police reports. He was desperate for me to help you, but I can't do anything unless someone is charged."

No one had ever been willing to charge Rose or her friends with the crap they did, no matter how I pushed. Now the shake really was coming back. I gripped the inside pockets of my pants and searched the crowd for Gabe. He had disappeared. More people were on the dance floor, some couples I didn't know, many girls I did. Rose laughed with a pair of her pals in the yard. The light from the party made her shadow long and threatening. Why a stupid slip of a girl scared me, I didn't know. Well, I did know. It was becoming all too much. Too many people, too much noise, too much stress....

A hand on my arm brought me back into the moment. Jamie stood beside me, looking concerned. "Everything okay?"

His words took a few seconds to sink through the layers I had been trying to build up against the crowd. Gabe had become my wall when he'd danced with me, but now he was gone and I was left flapping in the wind. Jamie handed me my jacket. I shrugged into it, pretending the shiver was from the cold.

"I have tea," he whispered to me, then hugged Hanna and kissed her on the cheek. "Where's Al?" His gaze found the pinup. "I see."

"Hanna wants to be my baby momma," I told Jamie, wondering how he'd react to the news.

He looked genuinely surprised. Either he was a really good actor, or she *hadn't* told him about it. "Really? Are you ready for babies, Hanna?"

"I have to be. I'm the only judge in the fifth division without a child. I'm hearing more and more that I can't make decisions involving children."

Jamie hugged her again, this time like the bone-crunching one he'd given me at school today. "I'm sorry, baby."

Hanna turned back to me once Jamie let her go. I huddled in my jacket and sipped at that awful tea. "Please promise me you'll consider my proposal? Jamie knows where to find me. I'm going to take Allie home. We're not the party type. But I did want to meet you." She glanced at Jamie. "In a normal sort of way."

"What's that supposed to mean?" I asked. Then I looked at Jamie and it made sense. He'd been bringing her reports for *years*. "You've been following me for years?"

He nodded like it was something every sane person did. "Sure."

Hanna gave my arm a polite squeeze and wandered off, taking the hand of her pretty girlfriend and disappearing toward the street while I glared at our shared brother. Jamie shrugged out of his oversized hunter-style jacket and dropped it on my shoulders. I glanced at him, then back at the crowd, who kept a wide berth now that Jamie was near.

"Where's Gabe?"

"Vampire thing."

I sighed. "And this is why we aren't exclusive."

"Don't be mad at him. He's a vampire. He can't stop being a vampire and ignore their politics any more than you can stop being a witch and ignore the Dominion. The Tri-Mega calls, he's gotta answer."

Yeah, but we were supposed to dance and be together at this terrible party that I didn't even want to attend. I couldn't say any of that, though, because it just sounded stupid and childish. "Your sister seems nice," I said instead. "Said you raised her."

"My mom was like yours in the parenting department, didn't know what she was doing. She still tries, of course. But I was the one to make sure Hanna got up for school every day, had food and clothes. Let her know that she'd get a hug if she needed one. I believe if my mother or your mother had had that when they were kids, they'd have treated us better."

Maybe. We strolled down the path away from the party. Could I get him to take me home?

"So that was Rose Pewette, Pillar of Earth." He sighed heavily. "Gabe told me some of the stuff she did to you."

"Doesn't matter anymore. I lived through it." She'd made me more determined to live through whatever life could throw at me. As much as I hated her, she'd made me a stronger person—though I still dreamed regularly of tying her to a chair in a room full of mirrors and hexing her with an ugly illusion spell.

"She had no right to do those things."

I waved it off. Rose wasn't important enough to waste time thinking about. "Did Gabe say when he'd be back? If not soon, can we go?"

Not like I'd find anyone to take home at a party full of girls, nor did anyone else even interest me all that much anymore. Maybe the tea and pills were doing other things to me. Gabe would have some idea how to whittle down the money-and power-hungry masses to help me find a suitable mother for my child. We didn't need a party for that.

Jamie was about to answer when a horrible ripping sound drowned him out. Something cracked in the distance. I felt the earth cry with a moment of shattering pain. A crash shook the ground and threatened to knock us off our feet, and many high-pitched shrieks blended into one. We turned back toward the patio in unison. I wondered if Jamie's expression was as horrified as mine was.

The grove of oak trees lay on their sides like toppled dominos —the end two broken in half as though they'd been snapped like crackers by giant hands. People were moving in a flurry, not sure what to do. Jamie gripped my arm and pulled me toward the edge of the driveway "Let's stay with the group. It's safer in public," Jamie whispered to me.

Safe was a weird idea since the trees had been dropped on the busy patio. It would take a pretty strong earth witch to tear the trees from the ground that way. We walked slowly around them, hearing the sirens in the distance. Some of the screams had faded off. A handful of elder Dominion members were trying to keep people away from the scene.

Giant bulbs of roots made the trees look like felled tops. I'd only seen anything like it from heavy rain and windstorms that would weaken the ground with water, then rip the trees out with straight-line winds. But we'd had neither lately. In fact, the summer and early fall were unusually dry this year. I wondered what witch at this party had enough power to pull a tree out of the ground like that. The earth didn't much like to give things back, so it would have been one hell of a tug of war. That was probably why two of the trees were cracked instead of toppled.

The third tree in the grove lay over part of the patio. Everyone kept trying to sneak a peek at that tree. Once we'd gotten to the edge of the crowd, I saw what so fascinated them. Much like in the *Wizard of Oz*, two feet stuck out from under the tree. They were clad in sparkling pumps with red soles, Louboutin, obviously. One was hanging half off, the other on. Rose Pewette's shoes.

CHAPTER 15

I was getting used to the whole police-suspicion thing. I sat on the edge of the planter box next to the house, waiting for their arrival and for Andrew Roman to come ask his questions. I knew it would be him simply because he wanted something from me that I refused to give. Not that I had all the details yet, but I was sure they'd come out in time. I'd turned down enough men in my life to know when someone took it personally.

The cops moved through the group questioning all the witnesses. My story had been short but precise, and Jamie's had been much the same. Neither of us had been close enough to see the trees fall. We had, in fact, been closer to the street than the patio as I'd been trying to convince him to take me home.

Roman quickly finished gathering his information and headed back my way. He pulled out handcuffs as he approached. Jamie rose to his feet, but Roman shook his head. "You can't stop it this time, any more than you could last time, Browan. Even his mom can't get him out of this."

"What?" I asked as he yanked me to my feet, pulled my arms behind my back, and cuffed me.

"Any weapons on you? Other than your magic?"

"I didn't do anything." I really felt like a broken record this time.

"So you keep saying. But half our witnesses are earth witches, and they all said they felt the wave of power come from this direction. Away from the party. Like near the street."

Tears began to cloud my eyes as Roman patted me down for weapons. But I really hadn't done it.

"I did it," Jamie said.

"Yeah, right, Browan. You can't save him from himself."

"He didn't do it! I did." Jamie closed his eyes and spread out a hand. The ground began to shake like a low-level earthquake.

People shouted. Cops screamed "Stop!" and pointed weapons in our direction. The earth quieted, and every law enforcement person in the area descended on us. On Jamie. They wrestled him to the ground—though he wasn't resisting—and slapped cuffs on him. I'd never seen anyone look as pissed-off as Roman did when he uncuffed me and shoved me toward my mom. I watched him stuff Jamie in the back of a police car and couldn't keep myself from shaking. Fuck, this was not how the night was supposed to go.

My mom gripped my arm and dragged me to the side to give me instructions on what to say to the cameras. It was a drill I'd practiced a thousand times. I knew nothing. I'd done nothing. I had no comment.

The circus of cameras that showed up made my head ache and my gut churn with worry. By the time I found a cab and got back to Gabe's apartment, it was after 2:00 a.m. I had called Gabe more than a dozen times, and it went to voicemail every time. I even left him a few frantic messages about Jamie being taken away. How long would it take for the Dominion to arrange Jamie's execution? Could we get him a trial? He was my brother, dammit, and I never had one before.

The most frustrating part was that I knew he hadn't done it either. I would have felt that kind of power coming from him.

And funny how it was aimed at Rose when I'd just been thinking ill of her. She couldn't have been all that powerful as Pillar since the earth didn't seem to care at all that she was dead. Usually if a Pillar died, there was a major catastrophe like an earthquake or volcano erupting. I had the TV on as background noise, but there was no mention of any major elemental upset, though quite a few stations spoke of her death.

What other options did I have if I couldn't get Gabe to help? No one would believe me when I said I didn't feel the power coming from Jamie unless I admitted to doing it myself, which would just set me up for execution instead. Hell, they'd probably just light us both up to save themselves the expense of investigating. I sighed and wiped the counter down, trying to think. Roman wanted something from me, right? He wanted me as a part of his group to represent something. I could do that. Maybe ask for something in exchange.

I dug through my stuff and finally found Roman's card. I rang him four times before he picked up. "What, Rou?" He sounded like he was at the police station and annoyed to be talking to me.

"Jamie didn't do it. I would have felt that kind of power coming from him. It had to have come from in front of us. I felt nothing before it hit, just the pain from the earth when the trees were ripped from it."

"Sure, there happens to be another rogue earth witch wandering around St. Paul. Two of you aren't enough?"

"He didn't do it. How do you know it wasn't someone from your group, the Ascendance?"

"No one would dare hurt a Pillar."

"Someone did."

"Are you confessing, Rou?"

I sighed and put my head on the counter. I missed Gabe, Jamie, and all of the people who had become such a constant pulse in my life. "What do you want from me? Really. And if I do what you want, can you help Jamie?"

The noise in the background died away. He was silent another minute before saying, "I can't free Browan. He admitted murder by magic. But I can offer you something else you want."

"What?"

"Santini."

"I already have Gabe, thank you."

"Where is he now?"

A sick feeling built up in my stomach. "What have you done with him?"

"He's fine for the moment. You have an address in your notebook. Come see me, Seiran Rou. Then we'll negotiate."

Address in my notebook? The address in Isanti for the Ascendance party? "It's almost an hour drive."

"Best get on the road, then, if you want Santini before the sun comes up." Roman hung up. I tried Gabe's phone again and got nothing. Dammit. Why did I have to choose? I growled at the phone and dialed my mom.

"You have to get Jamie out," I told her.

"Seiran, you must be reasonable."

"I am being reasonable. He didn't do it. And I swear, if you let him die for this, I will never let you see your grandchild."

"You're threatening me with a child that isn't even conceived yet to save a man you barely know."

"He's my brother. I realize that might not mean anything to you, but it does to me. You wanted a baby from me. I will have an heir, but I don't have to give you any rights. I can take that baby and move across the world."

She sighed. "I can only delay them so long. He admitted to murdering a Pillar with magic."

"Yeah, sucky Pillar. Where's the disaster to prove the earth cared?"

My mom's silence was enough of an answer. The earth had never recognized Rose even though the Dominion had.

"So you'll help Jamie?"

"You'd better give me a granddaughter, Seiran."

"I will work on it as soon as Jamie is safe!" I told her and hung up. Now I had to make sure Gabe was safe too. Damn him for being so quiet about whatever was going on in his life. Maybe if he'd talked to me about Roman, we could have avoided all of this.

By the time I got to my car—having to go back in twice for a coat and then keys—my heart was racing. The silence in the parking garage made the world so lonely. Funny, I'd never been a pack animal, but tonight I wished I were one. As I unlocked the car door with my old-fashioned key in the lock, arms snaked around me, taking me by surprise. Something pressed against my face, covering and burning my eyes and stinging my nose, while an arm like a vise wrapped around my arms and chest. I struggled for a few seconds before the bright pulses of my brain told me it wasn't going to let me struggle anymore. Darkness hit in a painfully unnatural sort of way.

CHAPTER 16

I woke up to what felt like a hangover: half-groggy, half-pained. The light behind my eyelids reminded me a lot of the white room of my mother's. Had I been drinking? I tried to recall the night and vaguely remembered the party. As I slowly opened my eyes, the world came into focus.

This room was more gray than white, with a few spatters of brown here and there. The stench hit me almost as fast as the realization that the brown was blood—old blood had a rotting-meat smell. I fought to keep my gorge from rising and tried to sit up. But much like in my mother's white room, I was strapped to a table.

The cold at my back told me it was metal, though the straps were pretty much the same. At least my head wasn't bound. A smaller table next to me had items like candles, matches, and sticks of incense. No smell would override the stink that permeated the room, though.

Only about ten by ten, the room had no windows, just one door. The door was solid-looking metal with a deadbolt on this side. Strange. I'd have expected it to be on the other side.

I reached out for any sense of earth and found it too far away to respond. Damn. Where the hell was I? Last night came back to me in a rush. Where was Gabe? Would Roman kill him? Had my mom been able to help Jamie?

The door opened with a whining squeak that made me close my eyes and cringe. Boots clomped toward me, and though I didn't want to, I opened my eyes to look at my captor.

Brock smiled at me in his ever-friendly way. He wore an old white wife-beater that had seen better days. "Hello, Seiran."

"Brock? What the hell? Did you do this? Let me go!"

He shook his head, grabbed a candle, and placed it at the top of the table above my head. "There's no other way, Seiran. It doesn't work from woman to man. Has to be man to man."

"What?" What was he talking about? Sex? "If you need a boyfriend, I can find you a few nice lycanthropes."

"I *need* your power."

"My power? And how the hell do you expect to get that?"

He gave me a sadistic smile. "The inheritance ceremony, of course."

"That only works for blood relatives."

Brock shook his head. "No, actually. That doesn't matter. I've done a lot of experimenting. It works from a female witch to another female witch or male to male. Or for a mix of sexes for blood relatives."

"So you plan to somehow make me say the words to give you my power and then kill me? Don't you think someone is going to catch on when you suddenly go from being a level-four fire witch to a level-five earth witch?" I struggled against the leather straps. He continued to place his candles.

"No one has caught on so far. They think it's some vampire hater. But vampires are so common now, I guess it's pretty easy to use them as a scapegoat. And I'm only a level four because that's what my mother was."

"You killed your mom? And I thought I was fucked up in the head."

He shrugged. "She was a real bitch. A lot like your mom, I bet. And like Rose Pewette."

"Did you kill Rose?"

"With a little help from the powers I stole from an air witch. I had to get you away from your protectors. Browan tried to take the bullet for you last time. I knew he'd do it again." He lit the first candle and began working his way around. "The Ascendance has done a lot of experimenting with the inheritance ceremony. They are all about making guys more powerful."

I knew there'd had to be something off about that group. "So where's Gabe?"

"No idea. Roman probably has him. He's obsessed. They had a fling or something back before they became vamps, and Roman hasn't forgiven Santini. He mentioned something about the Tri-Mega being involved."

Fuck! If something happened to Gabe, I was totally going to go apocalyptic on them all. "Brock, if you don't let me go, I'm going to do something awful to you."

He laughed. "You can try, but we're on a pier on the Mississippi. Underneath this concrete slab is water about twenty feet deep. Last I checked, you were an earth witch, not water."

"I suppose Kelly is in on this too." That would be just my luck, wouldn't it? Make friends with people who were trying to kill me.

"Nah, he's next on the list. Would have taken him sooner, but I've had my eye on you for a while."

I sucked in a deep breath and fought down the panic rising in my gut. "I won't say it. You'll kill me and still not get my power."

"Frank said that too."

"Frank wasn't a witch."

"Level-two earth. Probably why he hated you so much. All I had to do was whisper in his ear a little about how to take another witch's power, and he was all over it. The night I killed him, he wanted us to work together to take yours. Said you were a paranoid airhead who thought with his dick. Didn't you wonder why he was suddenly so interested in you?"

It made sense now, Frank's odd behavior and Brock showing up that night. "Bastard." Both of them.

"Aren't you happy I killed him?"

"I'd be happier if you let me go."

He bent over and pulled a large hunting knife out of his boot. "Let's begin the ceremony, shall we? Rituals 103. I know you have it memorized. I heard you are an excellent student. The professor was certain you were hiding how powerful you are. And she was right, wasn't she?" He walked around the table, speaking softly as he began the spell. "For balance and right be equal—"

"I won't say it." He could do most of the ritual himself. All he needed me to say was "my inheritance upon the grave."

The blade of the knife ripped into my left arm. Sharp pain sliced through me. Though the cut was fairly shallow, but he'd laid me open from mid-bicep to my elbow. I ground my teeth together and tried to keep from crying out, but I'd never been much of a masochist. Blood seeped from the wound. It pooled around my shoulder and arm. Air hit the cut, making it sting like nothing I'd ever felt before. I fought against panic. If I died here, who would save Gabe and Jamie?

"Chant with me, Seiran."

"Fuck you!"

He shoved the knife into the fleshy part of my right shoulder. The scream tore from me before I even felt it in my throat. He really was going to kill me. Could I make him do it without forcing me to say those words? Frank had been thoroughly broken on my doorstep. Professor Cokota pushed through my wards. She might have even been dead before that happened. The mess the wards made was probably a cover-up. How much torture had they endured before he'd finally killed them?

Gasping, I said, "You give me no motivation to say it. You're going to kill me anyway. Hurting me will only make me die quicker." I tried to breathe through the pain and not cry like a baby.

"You'll say the words. They all do. You want the pain to end faster, you'll say the words. If you say them now, I promise to make it quick."

I closed my eyes as his knife bit into my flesh again, this time my thigh. The world faded for a moment, but he slapped me back to consciousness. I was dizzy and the room was out of focus.

The verses were simple. Balance and gifting. The inheritance ceremony wasn't much different than the Pillar acceptance ceremony. The earth had never accepted Rose though she had still been Pillar. If the earth had accepted her, Brock would never have been able to kill her by dropping a tree on her. The goddess protected her own. If I could become the Pillar....

I wondered briefly if I could do it. Even this far away from the earth, if I were Pillar, I could shake the foundation of the world. If Gaea accepted me, she wouldn't let me die without a fight. She'd pour strength into me and maybe I could escape the stupid bonds and this nightmarish room.

The Dominion hadn't had time to choose a witch to replace Rose. I was level five. So as long as the earth didn't reject me, I could take that mantle. If the earth did reject me, it would kill me —but then it would be all over anyway.

But causing an earthquake in unprepared Minnesota would kill thousands. I wasn't worth the death of thousands. If the power of the Pillar fell to me, the Dominion would know it, and if I suddenly vanished again, they'd know someone killed me. But not who. Damn. What I really needed was Kelly. He could have pulled power from the water beneath the concrete, but probably would have drowned us all in his attempt to save us. I sighed. The Dominion really needed to train more male witches.

Then it all suddenly clicked, and I knew what I had to do. "I will say it," I told him.

"Then do it."

"I want something in exchange first."

Brock tapped the sharp end of the knife on the table. "What?"

"You. Fuck me." I'd seduced enough "straight" boys in my time to know that when Brock looked at me, he didn't see a friend or even just a vessel of power. He was attracted to me—and annoyed by that fact.

"I'm not gay."

I laughed, knowing how the sound made most react. He was no different. His spine stiffened and, yeah, a little bit south of the border did too. It was part of the natural competitive side of a jock. If I submitted to him, then he was still a manly man. Which was bullshit if I ever heard it, but if I could use that against him, I would.

"If I'm going to die, I'd rather it be during sex. You're an attractive guy. You can do me. I'll say the words, and then you kill me. We both get what we want."

"Frank was right: you are a total slut." He paused, then sighed heavily. "Men should not be as beautiful as you."

I shrugged, fighting to stay conscious. My blood ran sticky and hot from the series of cuts he'd inflicted, which didn't seemed at all attractive to me. How could I convince him? However, Brock put the knife down and began to unbuckle his belt.

"You are not going to get the right angle with me strapped down like this. Don't you want it to be *good*?" A deliberate blow to his ego.

He paused. "You just want me to let you go."

"Door's locked, right?"

He nodded.

"You're bigger and stronger than I am. You have more magic and have me locked in a room made of metal and concrete. I really don't see my advantage."

Brock undid the first restraint holding my chest and shoulders down. "You run, and I'm going to make you regret it."

Waiting for all the restraints to loosen was an exercise in patience that I sorely lacked. When they were all gone, I rolled over, cradling the cut-up arm more than the shoulder because it hurt more. The thigh was just a dull ache. He'd either made a shallower cut, or cut so deep I was going to lose the leg anyway. Sitting up hurt like hell. I pushed myself to the edge of the table, but Brock appeared in front of me with the knife.

I said, "Not going anywhere, baby. Just need help getting my pants off. You sort of did a number on my arms."

He glared suspiciously at me for a second before unbuttoning my bloody trousers and pulling them down my hips, lifting me a bit so they'd slide off. When he yanked them off the damaged thigh, I could barely contain my yelp of pain. Yeah, I guessed I wasn't going to lose that leg yet.

"I sort of expected you to be the commando type," Brock said staring at my Dolce undies. I'd worn them thinking Gabe and I would have a nice night in after the party. So much for that.

"Sometimes undressing is part of the seduction. Haven't you had anyone who wore sexy underwear just so they could take them off for you?" I struggled to unbutton the ruined shirt. Blood made the blue look brown. I hoped Gabe hadn't paid much for it. "If you come up here, I can ride you. Easier for both of us that way." Keep his mind focused on sex and maybe I had a chance. I ran through my memory of the inheritance ceremony in my head, fumbling only a time or two to remember the exact words and how the Pillar ceremony differed. Magic wasn't all about the words anyway. It was mostly about intent. Did Brock know that? I sure hoped not.

Brock pulled at the rest of the buttons and ripped off my shirt before climbing onto the table next to me. "I don't have any lube. But I do have a condom."

I raised a brow at him, trying to stop the shaking that had started in my hands and moved slowly into the rest of my limbs by focusing on my memory of the spell I needed to cast. "Thinking you were getting some tonight?"

"I'd planned to meet you at Santini's place after the party and seduce you. Frank said you went home with any man who offered to fuck you. But you were in such a rush, I had no choice but to take you by force." He kicked off his boots and shoved off his pants. His cock strained against his briefs.

"Glad he thought so highly of me." Both Frank and Brock.

Brock jumped down from the table long enough to strip off his briefs, then crawled back up. His cock jutted toward his navel. I wanted to pretend better than I currently was, but even thoughts of having Gabe fuck me couldn't wake my sleeping desire. Brock held the knife in one hand, condom in the other, and used his teeth to tear into the foil package before rolling it down his length. He tossed the empty package to the floor.

"You're shaking. Are you cold?"

No, I was pretty sure it was from blood loss and fear, but bringing that up might dampen his mood. "A little. I'm sure you'll warm me up."

He made to pull my underwear down, but I shook my head and grabbed them to keep them up. If I could keep his hands off me as much as possible, maybe I could survive this. "You're not gay, remember? Pull the back down, and you won't even know I'm a guy. I'm sure you've had girls that way before."

He nodded like it made sense, yanked the fabric off my ass, and lifted me to straddle his hips, facing him. He pressed his right hand to my bleeding left arm, then used my blood to lube up the condom. I shut my eyes and fought the urge to vomit on him.

"You are beautiful, you know. And I did like hanging around you on campus."

The head of his cock pressed against me, and the pain of his entry wasn't lessened at all by the fact that he was fucking me with my own blood. He might as well have gone in dry. I laid my head on his shoulder and let the shake take over my body as he thrust inside. It was not at all pleasurable, just hurt, so I tried to focus on the Pillar ceremony and divorce myself from what my body was doing. As though that was truly possible.

He began whispering the words to the inheritance ritual again, chanting in time to the rhythm of his thrusts. I followed the chant in my head, recalled all those classes in rituals and standard earth magics, and called to the earth that was so far away and yet so strong.

"Say it!" he growled at me. I clung to him, let him fuck me, and waited until he was almost at the end.

"When you come," I told him, breathing hard. Tears ran down my cheeks, but I wouldn't let him see them. I was just a thing for him to use, he couldn't really hurt me. Hadn't Matthew taught me that so long ago?

"*Fuck.*" He shoved into me harder, holding my hips with bruising force in both hands. The knife was lost at his side—which is what I'd been hoping for. I felt his body twitch in that final warning. "Say it!"

Then he was coming and clinging to me, trying to make it last. I whispered, "And to the earth I become the balance, strength, unity, and focus." I grabbed the knife and plunged it into his back as the power hit me.

He and I screamed together. The agony of the earth accepting me lasted only a few seconds—like being shocked by a billion volts of electricity, but it was enough time for Brock to recover. His punch threw me halfway across the room. I smashed into the wall with pain bursting up my spine and fell into a heap. Dizziness and nausea made the world threaten to go black.

The knife stuck from his back near his shoulder. They always made it look so easy in movies. Obviously I hadn't put enough force into it or even aimed it right. He leaned over the table and yanked the knife out.

"*Fuck!*" he screamed at me. "I knew you were up to something!"

I tried to sit up, move, anything, but the pain took me to the edge of that pit of life and death. I'd felt like this my first year in college when Rose had hexed my room. That night had been hours of hell, muscles and limbs twisted up in mind-blowing pain until the RA found me and undid the hex. Did I remember that hex? I thought about the words for a while, trying to think through the throbbing fog that surrounded me.

He came for me, knife in hand. I don't think he cared about the inheritance ceremony anymore. Could he steal my power and become Pillar? Probably not. But I'd pissed him off, so he wanted me dead anyway. That was clear on his face.

Finally I remembered the words of Rose's hex and knew I could do it. It might not stop him, but I could slow him down. I whispered the hex, directed it at Brock. He doubled up instantly, muscles retracting, contracting, like a full-body charley horse. The minor hex turned major because of the earth power channeling through me. He dropped to his knees, cursing enough to make a sailor blush, his grip on the knife so tight his knuckles were white. Still he struggled to reach me, growling and groaning like some snarling beast out for blood.

No wonder Rose had felt like a goddess. The connection to the earth was like some sort of utopia of peace and strength—a well of endless power. If she'd felt even a quarter of it as a level five earth witch she'd have felt like a goddess. And with the world acknowledging her as Pillar it wouldn't have mattered if the earth brushed her off. The balance of everything now hinged on me. I knew a little push one way or another, and I could cause some of the world's greatest catastrophes. Yet I couldn't even stop a college football player from killing me.

Brock writhed on the floor, crawling my way like a snake. Pain made it hard for me to think and hold the spell. Magic required focus and concentration, and pain did nothing but scatter thoughts in a million directions. For most, pain made it impossible to use magic. Brock had nothing but physical

182

strength, though, if he could reach me and kill me, his pain would stop. But I'd had years of practice enduring the viciousness of others to focus on finding the magic beyond.

When he finally reached me, he leaned against me, still fighting that pain. Yet the knife was rising, firmly in his grasp. Tears leaked from my eyes, and my body still refused to respond. Every bit of me hurt and for a minute I prayed his slash was true. But I didn't want to die. Not yet. I had a family now and a guy I was sort of into if I stopped fighting myself about it. Maybe I had a future. But like Gabe said, only I could make that decision.

I gave one final hard mental push into that hex, trying to stop his arm, and heard a loud snap.

Brock's eyes clouded over. The knife dropped from his fist. He collapsed to the ground. His spine bowed unnaturally. I let go of the hex, watched his whole body relax in death, and sobbed into my bleeding arm. It barely stung anymore.

For the first time in my life, I prayed the whole of the Dominion would find me. With Brock's empty eyes staring at me, I figured it didn't matter much at that point who killed me, so long as I got to say goodbye to those who mattered the most.

CHAPTER 17

I t's odd how sometimes unnatural unconsciousness brings rise to memories we thought we'd buried or lost in years of turmoil. My mind retreated to a happy place—the memory of my first date with Gabe. I'd badgered him for weeks before my birthday until he'd finally relented, and even then he said he we'd be going on the traditional sort of date. I had no idea what that meant. When he picked me up, I was wearing the tightest jeans I could find and a nearly see-thru shirt even though snow was falling and the temps were barely in the teens. I hoped the clothes didn't matter much and would be on the floor not long after the date began.

I wouldn't even let him pick me up from home. Instead I met him at a coffee shop down the street. I had already turned down a half dozen other guys when he parked his sports car at the curb and walked in looking like sex on two legs. I was so hoping he'd let me have him that night. Any which way he could want—I was willing.

His smile was wide and genuine, which just floored me. If he was so happy to see me, why did he keep turning me down? "You want to get a table or something to drink before we go?" he asked as he stepped up close, his hands in his pocket like he was afraid he was going to touch me.

I reached out, put my arm around his waist, and pressed my body against him. "We can go. I'm good."

His smile flickered a minute. He pulled away, taking my hand and leading me out the door. "You are."

His car was nice. I got in the passenger seat and strapped the belt on wondering if I could get him to head up the street so we could find a private parking spot and try out his big backseat. Sure he was sort of tall for that, but I was small and really flexible. We could make it work.

Gabe got in, turned on the car, and switched on the heated seats. Oh that was nice. He leaned over and kissed me lightly on the lips. I grabbed his neck before he could pull away and forced him into a deeper kiss. He sighed and seemed to release whatever tension he was holding because he kissed me full-on like he wanted to eat me. Fuck that was hot.

He finally broke the kiss, put on his seat belt, and pulled away from the curb. "Yeah, you're good."

"I can be even better," I promised him. "There's a lot up about two blocks that's always pretty empty."

"I'm not taking you to an empty lot for our first date."

"Might as well. No one gets a second."

"Ever?" He glanced at me.

I narrowed my eyes at him. What did he take me for? Some kind of breeder? "Never."

"You've never had sex so good with someone you wanted to stay?"

I shrugged. Sex was sex. It made me feel good for a while, but afterward my head would go nuts and I'd have to go anyway. Then I'd spend days worrying if the guy really thought I was any good or had just humored me. Not letting anyone have a second chance made it easier on me. "Nope."

Gabe nodded. "So if I took you to see a band or out to dinner or to dance or something, you'd get bored with me."

"Probably. I'd really like to have sex with you. I bet you're hung."

He tapped his fingers on the steering wheel as we waited at a light. "Maybe this wasn't a good idea."

"Why?" I reached over to caress his thigh. "I can help you with performance issues if you have them. I've done it before. It's okay if you bite me. I know vamps need blood."

He captured my roaming hand in his and held it at his side. "Will you do whatever I want tonight as long as I promise to have sex with you before we part ways this evening?"

"Sure. What the hell. Just know wining and dining me isn't going to matter. I'm already a sure thing."

"You're too young for wine." He pulled into the lot of a nice restaurant. I would probably be underdressed for it, but he didn't seem to care.

I didn't remember much about the food that night, though I know the staff had bent over backward to get anything that Gabe said we needed. I sat close enough to be practically in his lap and had my hand on his cock a good portion of dinner, though I did eat a bit and sip at the fake wine he had them bring me. He obviously didn't have performance issues since I could feel his erection through his pants, but his face was unreadable.

Finally I pushed the food away and climbed onto his lap. We were in the back corner anyway. The restaurant owners probably didn't want to see the slut that came in with the vampire. "Are you ready to go?" I rubbed my cock against his. "You feel ready to go." I leaned over and whispered in his ear. "We can pop into the bathroom real fast. I've got condoms and lube in my pocket. A nice place like this probably has good-sized stalls even in the guys' bathroom."

He lifted me off him like I weighed no more than a bag of marshmallows and got up. He tossed a couple bills on the table, grabbed my hand, and dragged me back to the car. Was he mad? He was so hard to read. Where was that smile we'd started the evening with?

Inside the car, he started it but didn't put it in drive. He stared straight ahead, hands gripping the steering wheel. I knew enough body language to know he was closed off. Okay, this was bad, right? I put my hands in my lap and glared out my window. What had I done wrong? Every other guy would have already been balls-deep in my ass by now and likely on their way to the rest of their night.

He began to say something, but shook his head and put the car in drive. The city passed by in complete silence. I didn't try to touch the radio and kept my hands to myself. I almost expected him to drop me off at the coffee shop, but we ended up in a parking garage below a unit of very expensive-looking condos. He turned the car off but didn't get out.

"So you wanna screw here?" I asked him. No one took me home to their place. Most of the time I got fucked in bathrooms or the backseat of someone's car. "I can suck you off. You won't even have to take me home. I can hitch a ride."

Gabe looked at me, his eyes dark in the fluorescent lights of the garage. A minute later he leaned forward and kissed me. Not the breath-stealing kiss like the first one we'd shared that evening, but this was more a sampling. He sucked my lower lip between his and massaged it with his tongue. It was odd. I'd never had a kiss like that before so I let him do it. He turned his head to the side and released my lip to slide his tongue into my mouth, not to duel, but more tentative. He grabbed my hands and ran little circles on the back of them with his thumbs, sending shivers down my spine.

I breathed in the scent and taste of him. The kiss deepened, but he kept a clear divide in the car, touching me and keeping me from reaching out to hurry things along. He broke the kiss briefly and rested his forehead against mine, sharing the same breath with me. It was oddly intimate, uncomfortable—yet not.

"I don't want to fuck you, Seiran Rou," he finally said. I began to pull my hands out of his grip but he held tight. "I'm going to make love to you tonight."

Whatever. He'd figure out fast enough that I didn't need the foreplay. I leaned forward to try to kiss him, but he wouldn't accept it. "Kiss me," I demanded of him.

He smiled that sweet smile I'd been waiting for. "I thought you didn't like kissing?"

"Most guys hate kissing. That's not weird."

Gabe captured my lips again in another long and searching kiss that made my cock so hard I could hardly sit still. Fuck. Who did that with a kiss? He smiled into my lips and said, "Then I think they're doing it wrong."

I tried to break free from his grip again. "Please," I whispered when he finally let me go. I unzipped his pants and for the first time had his hot cock in my hands. "Sweet Gaea," I mumbled, gripping his thick shaft. His expression barely changed, but he was obviously turned-on. Crap, I wanted to taste that so bad. He let me stroke him, but when I tried to bend over to suck him, he grabbed my chin and kissed me again. At least he reached across the seats to free my cock from the stupidly over-tight pants and rub me to his rhythm. I was going to come any second.

He teased me, stroking me until I was just this side of erupting, then giving me a slightly harder than comfortable squeeze to scale it back. I found it hard to concentrate on touching him between the kiss that never ended and his hands on my body. Somehow he'd short circuited my brain. All the guys I'd been with before and never once had that happened.

I clung to his shirt, unable to focus enough to actually touch him when my body teetered on the edge of coming. His rhythm kept me guessing, bringing me all the way to the verge and yanking me back again. I ended up in his lap. His hand still working me while I could feel the hot length of him pressed between us. Gabe worked his other hand down the back of my jeans, ghosting over my crease and finding the sensitive taint below. This time there was no edge—I was just soaring, coming so hard I saw stars and gasped like a fish for air.

My sight came back as my heart began to slow a little. I'd ruined Gabe's shirt and mine. Had I ever come so hard before? So much. I still sucked in air like I'd run a mile. Gabe kissed my neck and cheeks. He was still hard between us. I reached for him to get him off too. It was only fair. Maybe I couldn't be world-shaking good like he was, but I could give him some pleasure, right? Else he wouldn't be with me at all.

He captured my hands in his again and tucked himself away, eyes meeting mine. He was still so unreadable. We sat together like that for a few minutes, my heart still pounding, eyes locked as I tried to read him while he remained so stoic. He was probably pissed 'cause I was some kid he had to get off before getting down to it. I suddenly felt inadequate and tried to pull away.

He held me a moment longer and leaned in to capture my lips again. I let him, not sure what else to do. "Round one," he whispered.

"Huh?" I looked at him, trying to figure out what he meant.

"That was only round one. You promised to do whatever I want tonight. The night is far from over." He released my hands, pushed my already rehardening cock back into my jeans, and carefully zipped me up, then pulled a cloth out of his pocket and wiped at some of the mess on my shirt. He gave up a moment later and opened the door. Since I was sitting on him, I climbed out first. He followed, clicked the lock after he slammed the car door, and put his hand out for me. I took it, gripping it hard. Was he for real?

He'd taken me up to his loft and we'd had sex until just before dawn. I'd woken to a note on the pillow beside my head. The sun shined fiercely through the windows of his loft. I got that he couldn't stay, but somehow it still hurt. The night was done and so were we. But really, we weren't. He texted me the following afternoon and called me enough that I finally agreed to go out with him again. The sex was great, why not? For a while he made me not so lonely. And then when he was gone and the feeling returned, I convinced myself I didn't need him anyway. Until the next time.

It was a cycle that went on for years. He pushed and I pulled away. Would anything have changed if I'd run to him instead? I knew I was coming out of whatever unnatural sleep I was in because I could hear an annoying beeping and my gut hurt with some unspeakable fear that Gabe was gone and the cycle was over. Had Roman killed him? My heart ached with the possibility.

CHAPTER 18

Bright fluorescent lights brought back a world of bad memories. Thankfully the earth surrounding me was close and calm, ground cooling with the first hints of snow. I opened my eyes, despite the glare of brightness, and stared at a leafy ceiling. Was I in some kind of forest?

"Hey, are you going to stay awake this time?" a familiar voice asked.

I turned my head to look, expecting pain from the movement, but fortunately, it didn't hurt. Jamie sat in a chair next to the bed. A bunch of trees grew behind him, like some kind of indoor garden. He looked tired, but otherwise fine. He had his hair tied back in a ponytail, and a black sweater hugged his shoulders. Maybe I'd buy him some cashmere ones, since I didn't know if I could make myself hug him yet. Cashmere was a lot like a hug, minus the other body. Did brothers do that sort of thing for each other?

"But you were arrested," I said, my voice sounding like it hadn't worked in years. Had my mom got him out?

"Yeah. Thank you." He sounded sincerely thankful.

"But I didn't do anything. Couldn't."

"First guy in history to be the Earth Pillar." He gestured to the room. "Thus the elaborate accommodations."

Oh. Yeah. I wondered when they'd light up the fire pit.

The sun was setting. I felt the little things hunkering down for the night, plants and trees saddened by the loss of the sun, though willing to rest until it rose again. The door opened, and my mom stepped inside. She looked at Jamie, then at me. Closing my eyes, I prayed she'd go away. Surely she could wait until I was at least partially out of a hospital bed before she told me they were going to kill me.

Jamie scolded her. "You'll make his blood pressure go up. You know what the doctor said."

I heard my mother's heavy sigh. "Aren't the drugs supposed to help with that?"

They were both quiet for a while. Finally I heard my mother say, "Fine. Call me when he is feeling well enough to see me."

"That could be days," Jamie said. It sounded like she was moving toward the door, then it opened and shut.

"Weeks," I mumbled.

Jamie laughed. "Gabe will be here soon to take over. He'll keep the dragons at bay."

My eyes flew open at the memory. "Roman has Gabe!"

"What are you talking about? Gabe is fine."

"But Roman said he had him and told me to meet him in Isanti, or he was going to hurt him. Then Brock kidnapped me." And cut me up. I didn't even want to think about the sex. My idea, but it wasn't like I really had another choice. How fucked up was I that the only option I'd come up with was to seduce him? Why couldn't I have thought of the hex sooner? I was so stupid.

Jamie gripped my hand tightly. "I'm sorry I wasn't there to protect you."

I sucked in a deep breath and had to look away from him for fear I'd start crying. Give me a big brother and I had permission to be a baby? No way. "It's not your fault. You shouldn't have confessed to something you didn't do! Do you have any idea how I felt? I'd just found out you were my brother two hours earlier, and you were going to die."

Jamie looked a little ashamed. "For a while I thought maybe you did do it. Killed Rose, I mean. Gabe told me what she did to you. *I* wanted to kill her. Then Gabe came to bail me out of jail and said you were missing. Of course, that was after your mom called a shitstorm of lawyers down on the police department. What did you say to her?"

Before I could answer, the door opened and Gabe stood there in a U of M hoodie I'd bought him and tight jeans. Safe, sound, and one hundred and ninety percent drool-worthy. If I looked anything like I felt, I was a train wreck. Why did he keep coming back?

Jamie got up from the chair, stretched, and headed for the door. "I'll be back in the morning. No funny business. He's not well enough for that yet." He glared at me. "I mean you. I'm pretty sure Gabe's not the one with the overactive libido." He shut the door as Gabe moved to take his abandoned chair.

Once Gabe settled himself beside me, he began to rub the back of my hand in soft circles, which stirred things that had no right to be stirring while I felt this horrible. "You want me to talk?" he asked.

It was our usual ritual after I'd had some sort of incident at school. Usually we had sex, and then I would curl up in his arms, just listening to the sound of his voice. "Please."

"I love you."

Talk about dropping a bomb. He'd never said it before, always hesitated though I'd seen him start to say it many times. I'd have run from him before. Now I couldn't. Even if I'd had the strength, I didn't know if I would. I stared at him, waiting for more, but he shook his head.

Then why had he left me? "Where did you go? From the party, I mean."

He sighed and sat back. "I was hoping we'd talk about that after you were well enough to leave the hospital."

"Tell me now." The way he looked at me made my heart hurt more than anything Brock had done. "Are you leaving me?"

Gabe smiled, though it looked a little bittersweet. "I thought we weren't a couple?"

"But we could be." I could do it, couldn't I? For Gabe, at least. How many years had it been? Six, maybe seven? I suppose I could only push him away so much before he finally got the point. Just my luck that it was the same time I realized I needed him.

He crossed his legs and tilted his head, as though he couldn't see me right.

"Can we?" I repeated.

He sighed and frowned at me. So it was over, then. I felt tears burning my eyes. Dammit. Why had he come? Couldn't he just be a cold bastard and text me that it was over like every other asshole in the world?

Finally he said, "I could never leave you, Seiran. You've had me wrapped around your finger since you showed up at that Wisconsin Halloween party. But the Tri-Mega demanded I account for your actions. They thought you were a witch out of control and I was a master allowing you to do dangerous things. I had to face their inquiry."

The Tri-Mega. I knew only a little of it. "What does an inquiry include?"

"It's a lot like a trial. Someone supplies evidence against me, and I have to defend myself."

"Roman?" So that's why he was around. He had some sort of grudge against Gabe and I was just a means to an end. Hadn't he said as much himself when he'd showed up at my apartment after Frank's death?

"He and I have history."

"Like our history?"

"No. We were never lovers of any kind. His wife brought me

over—unwillingly—then killed a lover of mine. Roman thought I —we—seduced her. Doesn't matter what I say now, he still believes it. I killed her for murdering Titus, and Roman hates me for it."

"She killed your lover?" Why was I suddenly so jealous? The guy had been dead for a couple millennia; it wasn't like I had to compete. I just couldn't recall Gabe ever talking about another lover. He never dated that I knew of, though women and men threw themselves at him all the time.

He shrugged like it didn't matter, but there was a tightness in his shoulders. "It was a long time ago. You are my lover now. I even felt your pain—probably when you hit the wall. Your spine was bruised. I've had enough of your blood to feel that, miles away. I told the Tri-Mega you were badly hurt. If you hadn't been, it would have meant my death. As it is the inquiry will resume in a few weeks."

"Sounds a lot like the Dominion. So are we going to have matching pyres?" Exhaustion was beginning to pull at me. The pain seemed to numb me to the emotional stress, but I was happy Gabe wasn't going anywhere.

"No one is going to kill you, Sei. I've been telling you that for years. I won't let it happen. Jamie won't let it happen. Hell, not even your mother will let it happen, no matter what you think about her. The Dominion is busy rewriting about a hundred laws. You are Pillar. The earth accepted you. They can't deny what the earth has accepted."

"But I killed Brock."

Gabe leaned over and kissed me, lifting a hand to wipe tears from my cheeks. "They found traces of each victim in that room, including Frank and Julia Cokota. Roman said you called him, suggested someone in the Ascendance was involved."

"It was Brock. He killed his mom. Stole her power. Wanted mine too. Said he'd learned some things from the Ascendance about the inheritance ceremony and how it works for more than just blood relatives." Did the Dominion know that? Had they been purposefully hiding that?

Gabe nodded. "It's all over the news. He took some low-level witches who were involved with vampires to cast the suspicion wider. Kelly was on his list. Roman confiscated his computer from campus and found a detailed list of targets. He's been stalking you for two years." Gabe looked angry. "I should have seen it."

Except that Roman was with the Ascendance too, so did that mean he'd cover up whatever Brock's involvement was? I closed my eyes and mumbled, "Doesn't matter. I'm afraid of the world, remember? Everyone except you and maybe Jamie."

"I'm glad you trust Jamie. He's wanted that for a long time."

"You trust him," I told Gabe. "That's like gold to me."

He smiled that beautiful smile of his. Whatever he said in reply was lost. I fell asleep to him still massaging my wrist.

CHAPTER 19

Getting out of the hospital brought a circus down around me. My mom arrived to ward off the cameras. She was the star for all of them, taking the spotlight and answering questions. She actually smiled when Gabe took the wheelchair from her and helped me into his car. Her visits were minimal, though she did remind me of my promise to have an heir. I assured her I'd take care of it.

I spent several days recovering at Gabe's place, relaxing because I had a never-ending supply of books and Jamie turned out to be an adept apprentice in the kitchen. My left arm finally stopped aching, and though I still had to use a cane when standing for more than a few minutes, my back was healing. Apparently I'd suffered some sort of trauma that built up fluid around my spine and would heal in time. It could take weeks, months, or even years. The doctors were optimistic. I was just tired.

Kelly visited me with supervision. My paranoia was spreading. Jamie and Gabe seemed to have caught it, but I guess they had reason. Kelly left the Ascendance and officially joined the Dominion. His easy sense of humor made me like him despite all my lingering issues. He hadn't known Brock that long and was a little weirded out by the fact that he'd been on a hit list.

Hanna came to tell me of her confirmed pregnancy. I'd figured since I'd been in the hospital anyway, getting it done would make my mom happy. Pictures of the microscopic blob didn't mean much to me, but they meant a lot to Hanna, Allie, Jamie, and my mother. Maybe when the kid didn't look so much like an amoeba, it would finally sink in that I was going to be a father. It still felt sort of unreal.

The Dominion ruled my use of a level-five hex to be in self-defense. My punishment was to teach a class in magic-based defense, including wards, counter-hexes, and counter-curses. The latter two were not some of my strengths, but Jamie helped me study. He seemed to have a good grasp of the defensive magic —all self-taught, of course.

The night of the Tri-Mega inquiry arrived. Gabe waited with that endless patience of his for me to dress and hobble to the door. I left the cane behind. No need to let a powerful vampire see me as weaker than I was.

I knew a little about the Tri-Mega. The three most powerful vampires in the world ruled with an iron fist. Not even the Dominion could affect what they decided. Having personal experience with Gabe and knowing how powerful he was, then thinking about how crazy-strong the Tri-Mega must be scared the shit out of me. I knew how to finesse the Dominion. This was a whole other world.

"Is there a code to follow? Something we can find a loophole in?" I asked Gabe, who sat like a statue in the driver's seat.

"Nothing like the Dominion has. Just a set of basic rules."

"So what are you in violation of?"

"I've been accused of trying to set up a nest without going through the proper channels."

I had to shift in my seat to look at him, but couldn't help saying what I thought. "Like a bird?"

He laughed lightly. "Not really. It's a group of vampires who exist under one leader. A nest has at least ten vampires, a human focus, and a master like myself."

"So I'm your human focus?"

"There is that accusation."

"But we don't have ten vampires. Does Mike count?"

"Mike is the only vampire I created who lives in the city." Gabe passed another car on the freeway and took the ramp off.

"Oh. Have you created enough vampires to make a nest?"

"Yes. Though again, Mike is the only one in the city. And it's not like I'm having a casting call. Hell, it's been more than two hundred years since I brought anyone over." We pulled into the parking garage of an upscale hotel. "We're only meeting with Tresler."

"So, just one of the three most scary vampires in the world. No pressure, eh? What do you want me to do?"

Gabe gripped my hand and said, "Just answer him honestly."

Since we were meeting at the hotel restaurant, I doubted we'd have any sort of smackdown here. Though I guess if a vampire wanted you dead, it didn't matter where you were. Sort of like the Dominion.

For a very powerful vampire, Tresler really just looked like an ordinary man. Good-looking in a Richard Gere circa *Pretty Woman* sort of way. Salt and pepper hair, muscular beneath the expensive suit, and stiff in the face, like he didn't smile much. He had a shark-like presence that made me nervous.

The waiter arrived and filled our glasses with a thick red wine. I didn't care for red, but I could pretend with the best.

Tresler took a sip of his wine. "Hello, Mr. Rou. Do you know why you're here?"

I shrugged. "Someone is saying untrue things about Gabe."

"What is untrue?"

"He's not making a nest."

"You are not his focus?"

"I don't know what that means."

Tresler put his glass down. "I ordered something for you. Humans are fascinating. Will you eat?" The waiter brought a plate of steak and vegetables to the table. He bowed and left us in privacy.

I stared at the meat. The weight of anxiety in my stomach made it hard to even think about eating. A glance at Gabe told me I should at least try. I picked up the fork and nibbled at the veggies.

"How about I put that question to you, Gabe?"

"I've already given that answer."

"I'm asking you again."

Gabe sighed heavily. "He is my focus. He is my purpose for living. Will I someday exchange blood with him to make him mine forever? That is for him to say."

Exchange blood? "You mean, like, make me a vampire?"

Tresler smiled that hungry smile of his. "A focus is the living side of a vampire pair. You'd be bound to him for the lifetime of your vampire. His servant, if you prefer the term, though you'll have more freedom than those we just use for food. We consider those to be thralls. A focus is more of a commitment. He would share his power with you, and you would share your life with him. Most of us prefer to be bound to lovers rather than servants. Forever is a long time to be stuck with someone you hate."

Now I *really* wasn't hungry. Gabe wouldn't look at me. "Forever?" My voice sounded like a squeak.

"I wouldn't do anything without your permission, Seiran. It's like the inheritance ceremony. You have to speak the words and willingly take my blood." Gabe glared ahead like something interested him out the far window.

Was Tresler doing this on purpose? Trying to break us apart? I shoved the plate of food away. "So what's with the inquiry?" I asked Tresler. "I'm not bound to him. He doesn't have a bunch of vamp groupies. What's the deal?"

"You killed a man recently, with magic. Why?"

It seemed like an odd question, though I'd asked myself the same thing a thousand times. "Because he was trying to kill me."

"And why did you need to live?"

Good question. "He killed for power. If he took my power, he would have hurt more people."

"But if you'd died without letting him take your power?"

I looked at Gabe, who was emotionless and still beside me. "It would have hurt some people."

"So you saved your own life to keep from hurting other people?"

"I didn't want to die. Not without saying goodbye to the people I care about. But it's not like Gabe told me to do it or anything. He promised. He won't compel me to do anything. I trust him."

"If you were truly bound to him, he would not have that power over you. He has more power over you now."

"But *bound* sounds like a commitment, and I've got commitment issues. That's not news to anyone."

"There are those who say you care for none."

"They'd be wrong. I care about Jamie. He's my brother. And Gabe." Gabe sat so still, like he could disappear from the room if we didn't notice him. "He thinks I'm beautiful, even when I'm ugly. He kisses me like I matter. Loves me even when I can't love myself."

"And how do you feel about him?"

"He..." *is someone I couldn't live without.* When I thought Roman was going to hurt him, I'd panicked. Gotten myself hurt and nearly died trying to get back to him. "I think he's always beautiful. I love him."

A look of shock crossed Gabe's face. Was that the wrong thing to say? "I'm sorry," I whispered, staring at the untouched meat on my plate. If I tried to eat it now, it would probably come back up, and somehow I didn't think that would impress the super-vamp sitting with us.

"If I dismissed all charges right now, what would you do?" Tresler asked.

"I'd probably go home and ask him to fuck me senseless."

"No focus bond?"

I picked at the summer squash. It was wilted, and I wondered if they'd overcooked it or it'd just been bad to start. Wrong time of year for summer squash. "Is that required? I'd rather just have sex and cuddle a little."

Tresler chuckled. "Take your witch home, Santini. Best you keep him away from your enemies until you both decide to take the next step. And put in a registration form before you start to nest."

Gabe took my hand and led me back to the car without saying anything. He didn't even look at me. Had I messed up again? The bruises were going away, so the pretty outside was still mostly intact—with a few scars added. And no one knew better than Gabe just how messed-up and ugly I was inside. When he made no move to start the car, I really worried.

"Gabe?"

"Say it again," he said quietly, hands in his lap, eyes on the steering wheel.

"What?"

He closed his eyes and shook his head. "I love you," he said. I didn't even flinch this time when he said it.

"I love you too," I told him.

"Messed-up insides and all."

I laughed. "No one is more messed up on the inside than me. But yeah, I love all your messed-up insides too. Now take me home and fuck me."

"I will make love to you."

"That's okay too."

He leaned over to kiss me, tears glistening at the edge of his eyes. I kissed him promising things to come. The new moon would begin in less than a week, and he'd promised me a vacation full of him, power, and sex. Life really couldn't get much better.

Join the mailing list and download the exclusive free short story WitchMinion.

The story continues with Reclamation, download now.

RECLAMATION

PROLOGUE

The cold crackled through the forest like glass shattering, rendering all else silent in the dark. The trees stretched skyward, their barren branches a testament of their will to survive even the most brutal temperatures. Everything else hid away seeking safety.

Find shelter. Get warm.

My paws froze and stung, turning numb from the bitter chill. Even my heavy coat couldn't keep the cold from freezing me to the core. I staggered but kept running. The forest had changed. It was not the sanctuary I'd bonded with these past few years. Gone was the soft embrace I'd come to crave and the gentle, welcoming touch of Mother Earth's power.

Yet I kept moving with no direction to my flight. Just an onward movement that meant distance. No matter how hard I tried, I couldn't outrun the past or the pain.

Confusing memories from a different life swirled inside my head. Bloody flashes and the expression on his face—betrayal?—refused to let the earth steal humanity from me. I wanted to lose myself in the animal and forget that I'd ever been human.

Find shelter. Get warm, the voice in my head persisted.

His heart had stopped beating under my hands. Blood had heated my skin and stained me with something that could never be removed. Breathing had become almost impossible when his eyes had clouded over. His death, my madness.

How many days had I wandered, teetering between this life and the animal nature I sought to alleviate the grief? Every once in a while I could hear the howl of the dogs pursuing me, scent them in the distance as they were ready to rip me limb from limb as penance for my crime. The Dominion, Tri-Mega, the Ascendance, and probably the humans too, all seeking my death.

I deserved it, having killed everything I loved. I prayed for death. That would stop the pain, right?

Find shelter. Get warm.

A dark farmhouse in the distance beckoned as a possible break from the bitter cold. It was shelter. Might not be warm, but my gut wanted me to obey the voice. Hopefully no one was home else I'd be forced to hurt people again just to escape. I trotted around the house and discovered the scent of humans was old. If any had been there, it had been weeks, maybe even months earlier. I carefully slipped inside and forced myself to shift back to human flesh.

My skin ached like cold fire burning through my extremities. Fur was warmer, the lynx more prepared for the cold, and though this form was bigger, it felt small, compact. Too small to hold everything I had been and keep the pain from leaking through. Emotions rained down like golf-ball-sized hail. There was no stopping the tide this time. A human brain had far too much capacity for thinking, blame, anger, and self-loathing.

I cowered in the corner, curled around myself, crying, freezing, unable to find the motivation to keep going. My heart ached with accusations of murder.

Get warm. Find food. The voice's demand changed. Was I hungry? I was still cold, but that was only fair, right? *He* would be forever cold, alone. I'd hated to leave him.

The farmhouse was silent but mostly clean. The water ran, and the thermostat sat at an even sixty degrees. The fridge was barren, but a heavily loaded stand freezer and well-stocked pantry proved this was more of a vacation home. I pried open the tab on a can of peaches and wolfed the fruit down. My stomach growled like I'd swallowed my lynx instead of just changed shape.

When had I last eaten? Days ago, probably. Without him, none of the mundane things mattered. The thought of him brought a rise of nausea and the memory of his last moments. I shoved the can aside and found my way to the only bathroom, and had to fight my rebelling stomach when it wanted to force up the fruit. I gagged and refused to let go of the food I ate.

You need to eat, the voice in my head told me, but I couldn't.

A scalding shower washed away some of the dirt but none of the grief. Wet footprints followed me like his ghost had latched on to me as I searched the house for warmth and comfort— neither of which I deserved. A chest in the upper bedroom held flannel shirts that I could wear like an old-style nightdress. They smelled a little musty, but heat was more important. Would the shivering ever stop?

There was a vague memory in the back of my brain that reminded me I'd had the shakes before this. From cold? Did that mean I was always cold?

The reflection in a dusty old mirror was not kind. My hair was shorn close to my scalp, eyes shadowed in deep black hollows with the lack of sleep only days could bring. My weight had dropped, giving me more of a sallow complexion and a gaunt stretch to my face. Gone was the beauty he'd spent years coveting. He likely would have turned me away now anyway. Better that he was gone, right?

I sobbed. Was this what I'd become? Some kind of fugitive?

Earth Pillar. I laughed bitterly through the tears. That hadn't changed anything. Love didn't conquer all. Gabe was dead. Jamie probably was, too, since I'd shot him. If I had any sense of justice

at all, I'd pull the rifle out of the closet—I smelled the gunpowder
—and off myself right now. Maybe it would lessen the pain, but
then, I didn't really have a right to stop my suffering after what
I'd done to them.

My hands shook so hard my fingers were numb. I couldn't
find the strength to reach for the end, despite the tears, the
memories, and the loneliness. *Rest. Things will be better when you
wake.* I curled up in the foreign bed and cried myself to sleep,
wishing for the chance to just feel his arms around me one more
time.

I love you. Sleep.

The story continues with Reclamation.

LETTER FROM LISSA

Dear Reader,

Thank you so much for reading *Inheritance*, the first book in the Dominion series!

Be sure to join my Facebook group Lissa Kasey's Mystical Men, for fun daily polls, writing snippets, and updates on new releases to this series and others. For a sneak peek at my work before it's published join my Patreon group. Patrons receive three new chapters a week and many other perks. For monthly updates on what's coming out and character shorts subscribe to my Newsletter. Also check out my website at LissaKasey.com for new information, visiting authors, and novel shorts.

If you enjoyed the book, please take a moment to leave a review! Reviews not only help readers determine if a book is for them, but also help a book show up in searches.

Thank you so much for being a reader!

Lissa

ABOUT THE AUTHOR

Lissa Kasey is more than just romance. She specializes in in-depth characters, detailed world building, and twisting plots to keep you clinging to the page. All stories have a side of romance, emotionally messed up protagonists and feature LGBTQA spectrum characters facing real world problems no matter how fictional the story.

ALSO BY LISSA KASEY

Also, if you like Lissa Kasey's writing, check out her other works:

Simply Crafty Paranormal Mystery Series:

Stalked by Shadows

Marked by Shadows

Kitsune Chronicles:

Witchblood

WitchBond

WitchBane

Survivors Find Love:

Painting with Fire

An Arresting Ride

Range of Emotion

Hidden Gem Series:

Hidden Gem (Hidden Gem 1)

Cardinal Sins (Hidden Gem 2)

Candy Land (Hidden Gem 3)

Benny's Carnival (Hidden Gem 3.5)

Haven Investigations Series:
Model Citizen (Haven Investigations 1)
Model Bodyguard (Haven Investigations 2)
Model Investigator (Haven Investigations 3)
Model Exposure (Haven Investigations 4)

Pillars of Magic: Dominion Chapter
Inheritance (Pillars of Magic: Dominion Chapter 1)
Reclamation (Pillars of Magic: Dominion Chapter)
Conviction (Pillars of Magic: Dominion Chapter)
Ascendance (Pillars of Magic: Dominion Chapter)
Absolution (Pillars of Magic: Dominion Chapter)

Evolution Series:
Evolution: Genesis

Boy Next Door Series:
On the Right Track (1)
Unicorns and Rainbow Sprinkles (2)

Printed in Great Britain
by Amazon